EYES OF MIDNIGHT

Eyes of Midnight

AN INLAND SEA NOVEL

Shanon L. Mayer

Shanon Mayer

First Printing, 2023

Cover design by JD&J Design

ISBN: 9781958076057

Published by Shanon L. Mayer, Vancouver WA 98663
https://shanonlmayer.com

For everyone who helped to make Dragon Keep the magical place it is today. Thanks for everything.

Books by Shanon L. Mayer

Chronicles of the Chosen
Sphere of Power
Veil of Deception

Jen Rice novels
Captives and Prisoners
Festival of Souls

Inland Sea
Star of Darkness
Eyes of Midnight

1

"Hey Wendi, we're running low on chupacabra blood again." Crucian stepped around one of the low counters that were scattered throughout the shop. He bumped into a barrel of griffon feathers but caught it before completely overturning it, still managing to dump a handful of brown and gold feathers onto the floor in the process.

"Do we any have more in the storeroom downstairs?" Wendi called over to him, almost thirty feet in the air on a rickety ladder, holding onto the shelf in front of her for dear life. Much as Wendi liked Crucian, the guy couldn't walk through the shop without crashing into something. Now, it looked like he was headed for the ladder she was standing on and the last thing she needed was to fall into the ever-brewing potions that Phemie tended to leave scattered everywhere.

Wendi was the owner of Dragon Trading, a store located in Dragon Keep in the Inland Empire which specialized in rare and difficult-to-obtain goods. She had opened the shop a few years before, mostly by accident. Not welcome in most towns she went to; she had been in need of a place that was private and out of the way and Dragon Keep had fit the bill perfectly. She bought the keep at a discount since it had been abandoned for almost fifty years, with the sole intention of remodeling it and living there.

Unfortunately, remodeling and maintaining a keep as large as hers had required a lot more money than she'd had available. She had spent some time debating before opening the shop but in the end the answer had been obvious. Using some of the junk left over from the last time she had gone out wandering and hadn't been able to offload anywhere else, plus a handful of her own special recipes, she had stocked the shelves of the one storefront she had cleared and declared herself open for business.

Not that any of it was really junk; a lot of it was just stuff that everyone else was already carrying.

Except for her recipes, of course. Those were personal.

Three other people lived and worked at Dragon Keep alongside Wendi, including Crucian, who was really handy when Wendi needed an extra burst of strength or to test out a new concoction when she was unsure about its effects. She was pretty sure that Crucian had some troll in his background, not because he looked particularly trollish, but because he has some features that raised suspicion in a sufficiently critical mind.

At almost seven feet tall, he was far too tall to be purely human, for starters. He had turned up as a full-blooded human in all of the tests Phemie had done on him but Wendi still had her doubts. His arms were too long for his body, as were his legs. Both of those caused him to walk slightly stooped over, as though the air at his head level was much heavier than the air where the rest of the population walked. Both of those features could be easily overlooked and written off as natural anomalies, were it not for the fact that the guy regenerated.

Humans just don't do that.

"I just looked down there," he called up to her, holding up an empty barrel and shaking it upside down over his head. "It's empty." Wendi winced at his action; the last time he had overturned a barrel over his head, it had turned out to be not quite as empty as he had believed and it had taken them the better part of the day to remove the sap that subsequently covered his body.

Also living at Dragon Keep was Phemie, who was barely over five feet tall with light brown hair that usually had bits of feathers, wooden beads, or other trinkets dangling from it. She was also the most talented witch Wendi had ever met. She was one of the best at identifying spells and forecasting what the effects of new magical items would be.

Phemie was the one that brewed up all of the magical potions and decided which items should be stocked on the shelves as components and what didn't need to be there.

Except poisons; she left those for Wendi.

Phemie was the person who had sparked Wendi's interest in carrying the exotic and rare goods that her shop now specialized in. Until meeting Phemie, Wendi had believed, as most people did, that magic just happened. Someone who happened to be trained in the magical arts waved their hands or pointed a little stick and magic happened.

It wasn't that easy.

"Magic is a process," Phemie had explained patiently. "Much like cooking a cake or making a new pair of shoes. Each of these takes ingredients and a decent amount of skill to put the ingredients together in the right order.

"Done correctly, you'll have the deliciously delectable treats that make a baker famous and the fabulous fashions that serve the ranks of royalty.

"Done wrong, however, you get a disgusting disaster."

That philosophy, in a nutshell, was where Dragon Trading's success came from. While paper, quills, candles, ink, whetstones, fishing hooks, and lamps could be found at just about any shop in any town a person could wander into, there weren't many places that specialized in the harder-to-get components that mages always needed. In most places throughout the Inland Empire, magic users had to go out and find the components they needed for their spells all on their own. A handful of mages from the Academy at Three Rivers, students all, had discovered that the shop at Dragon Keep carried a lot of the magical supplies that they needed and word began spreading.

So quickly had word spread, in fact, that it appeared they'd run low on chupacabra blood.

Again.

Then there's Jaegar. When Wendi first met him, she thought that he was just another standard human, even if he was a bit slow-witted at times. Jaegar had light brown hair with streaks of blond shot through it and bright blue eyes. He also had a tendency to run into walls and his explanation was always that he forgot to use the door.

It had been Phemie that discovered that Jaegar was actually an ogre, transmutated into a human with a spell that was strong enough that even Phemie hadn't managed to come up with a cure for it yet.

Secretly, Wendi believed that inability was deliberate on Phemie's part, although she'd never tell her friend she thought so. The only thing more dangerous to the structure of a building than a human who forgets he isn't an ogre anymore is an ogre who forgets he isn't human anymore.

With a sigh, Wendi carefully climbed down the ladder, keeping one eye on Crucian to make sure he wasn't moving. "I'll go look," she said once terra firma was within reach. "There should be another cask of it down there."

"Phemie said she used a bunch of it last week," he called after her as she headed for the stairs.

She'd forgotten about that. Chupacabra blood was one of the main ingredients in Phemie's camouflage potions, mostly because of the obnoxious critters' ability to blend in with their surroundings. The shop had run low on that particular variety of potions the week before so of course Phemie had used a bunch of it to brew more.

Handy as a chupa's skill at hiding was when it came to potion brewing, it made it that much harder to go out and capture the cursed things.

"Fine." she took a couple steps to the side and scooped up the feathers that he had spilled onto the floor. "I'll see if anyone's heard of another one around here somewhere."

"There's supposed to be one out in Landor," Phemie supplied as she flew into the room. Phemie, always original, didn't use a broomstick like other witches. Particularly inside the shop it just wasn't feasible; she would crash into everything even more often than Crucian did. Instead, she'd enchanted an overstuffed, hideously green colored lounge chair to fly her around to where she needed to go. It just didn't get more than six inches off the floor, which was much more manageable as far as Wendi was concerned.

"I'm assuming you're talking about the chupa."

She landed in a small open area of the floor near the back of the shop. "I started looking into that as soon as I knew I'd be using the last of it and heard tell that there's a bunch of goatsucker sightings out that way." She wore her standard uniform of a loose, flowing black dress. That day's particular one was spotted with small silver sigils, magical markings that had been stitched to the fabric of the skirt.

Wendi hadn't ever asked why she wore clothes like those, nor did she ask why she had so many sigils tattooed onto her chest, arms, legs, pretty much anywhere but her face.

The main reason Wendi didn't ask about things like that was because she didn't want Phemie, or anyone else for that matter, to ask the same kinds of questions about her. Why Wendi had black, pupilless eyes, for example, or where the rough scar that ran from her left cheekbone and covered most of the lower left side of her face and neck came from. There were just some questions for which she didn't have answers, at least not easy ones.

"I'll head out that way in a couple days or so, then." If Wendi had been going out after something larger than just a goatsucker, she would have brought more of the group with her but she wouldn't need them for this. Besides, Jaegar would just scare the skittish things off and Wendi would have to go out and track them while they were hiding. No reason to make her job any harder than it already was. "Can you mind the shop while I'm gone?"

It was a ridiculous question; she knew it as soon as she asked. Phemie was probably more capable of taking care of the shop than Wendi herself was.

Early the next morning, Wendi had Crucian help her load a handful of supplies into her travelling wagon. Crucian and Jaegar had built the wagon for her to use when she went out to gather fresh specimens and it had quickly become mandatory for her to use while travelling. It had a wooden frame on it with huge timbers that were strong enough to hold up all but the largest creatures while she worked on them. Multiple hooks lined each wall of the wagon, attachment points for her to secure anything that she needed to transport while she was out.

This wagon was slower and a lot more ungainly than her regular wagon but it had proven invaluable so there was no way she was going to go hunting without it. Landor was over thirty miles away and even though chupacabras were relatively small creatures, they were vicious and sneaky, more prone than most creatures to escape whatever binds she could put them into, so she wasn't about to even attempt to lug one that far intact.

Thankfully the bitterly cold weather of winter had relented and the air, while still crisp, was clear and there weren't many clouds in the sky to disrupt what little warmth the sun was able to provide. There were a handful of small animals out along the way, mostly rabbits and other early risers that didn't mind the cold. It was almost noon before the thin layer of frost completely dissipated and even the residual water didn't last for very long.

When the outlying buildings of Landor appeared on the horizon, Wendi pulled the hood of her travelling cloak up to cover her head. The scar that covered part of her face didn't bother her much, it had stopped hurting about two years earlier, but it still bothered other people who saw it. They always asked the inevitable questions and there was no good way for Wendi to explain that she didn't know where it came from.

She had ideas, of course. She'd come into close contact with more spells and poisons in the last five years than most people did in a lifetime. Any one of the explosions that had occurred, the result of incorrect mixtures in her laboratory, could have resulted in damage similar to what she had received.

Even more disturbing to other people than her scars were her eyes. Someone came up with the ridiculous idea long ago that a person's eyes were the windows to their soul, or some such nonsense. Since then, everyone automatically assumed that Wendi's soul was every bit as devoid of light as her eyes.

For both of these reasons, she kept her hood pulled tightly against her face as she entered town. The fabric of her cloak was heavy enough to keep heat in but the weave was loose enough that it didn't impair her vision regardless of how low she pulled her hood.

As with most towns in the area, Landor was comprised of loosely gathered buildings and a handful of small farms scattered along the outer edge. There was the standard baker, general store, weaver, and a handful of other small businesses scattered through the town, but what caught her eye immediately was all of the posters lining almost every wall, tacked onto every hitching post, and scattered everywhere her eyes fell. Curious, she climbed down from the wagon and walked over to investigate.

"Reward," the posters promised. "For information regarding the whereabouts of the missing slaves from Basch."

She felt her breath catch in her throat as she read the words. If there was one thing she couldn't stand, it was slavers. Those people, in her opinion, were the ones devoid of a functioning soul. Life was precious, a valuable thing, and for people to be traded like cattle was the ultimate offense.

She snatched the paper from the wall, then the next, then the one after that, furious that the people of Landor would allow such a thing to be posted in their town. She began to wonder if some of the residents secretly supported the slave trade. If so, she would have to reconsider her opinion of the small town. Soon, she had a small stack of the offensive papers in her hand and noticed that a few of the townspeople had begun looking at her strangely.

No surprise, Wendi thought to herself. Her hood had slipped as she frantically removed the notices. She felt their stares piercing her skin like tiny daggers but rather than giving them the satisfaction of seeing her act irrationally any further than they already had, she shoved the stack of posters into the pocket of her cloak and strode off towards the general store.

"Can I help you find something?" a voice called out to her from behind the counter. The voice came from a tall but portly man, easily in his fiftieth year. Even as he inquired, Wendi could still feel that there were still plenty of strange glances in her direction as she perused the dust-filled shelves of the store, so it took her a few moments to figure out what she was looking for. Why was she there?

Right, she was supposed to be looking for a chupacabra. It had been almost a year since the last time she had tracked one, now she just needed to remember how she had done it then. "Do you know where I can find a goat?" she asked as she turned her obsidian eyes on the shopkeeper.

His eyes widened when he met her glance and he took a step backward. "A... a goat?" he repeated. "Why do you want one of those?"

"I'm looking for a chupacabra," she explained. Most of the town had already seen her face so there wasn't much point in trying to hide it any longer. The smaller the town, the faster the gossip spread. She had learned that from years of experience. Anyone who hadn't seen her directly would likely be informed of her presence within the hour. "They like goats." It wasn't an understatement; goats were the preferred snack of chupacabras everywhere, as far as Wendi had been able to tell.

They were called goatsuckers for a reason, after all.

"You can get one from my nana's farm," a small child at the end of the counter spoke up. He looked at her directly, without any of the fear or hesitation that Wendi knew would develop with age. "She has lots of goats."

2

There was a reason Wendi didn't like goats. They were mean, filthy, smelly animals that seemed to take perverse pleasure in doing exactly what you wanted them not to do. The one she had purchased that evening for three silver sheckles was no different, refusing to walk where she wanted it to go. It had no intention of leaving its home farm willfully, so the only way she could get it to where she needed it to be was by tying a rope from the goat to the wagon and forcibly pulling it.

"Come on, you stupid beast," she called out to it as it bleated contentiously behind the wagon. It left deep gouges along the ground as they went, digging its hooves into the packed dirt and refusing to budge. "Should've brought something to knock it unconscious until we got there," she grumbled.

She brought it a few miles out of town, hoping that she was at least heading to the right area. Phemie had said that the chupacabra was to the northeast of town but Wendi's sense of direction was not always the most accurate of her senses. Finally, she found a small clearing that would work and unhitched the goat.

Immediately, the goat tried to kick at her with both hind hooves, but she was expecting that and stepped easily out of the way. With a heavy iron spike, she tied its lead to the ground so it couldn't escape, sidestepped its attempted ramming of her, and moved the wagon so that it was out of sight. She could never be sure how a chupacabra – or any other beast, for that matter - would react to the wagon's presence, so it was best to keep it out of sight until she needed it again.

That finished, she settled into the tall grass to wait. Chupacabras were patient and wary creatures, so she knew that it would be a number of hours before one would answer the goat's bleating call. She was on a low hill, sloping from tall trees above to a bubbling stream at the bottom. A few birds called, arguing or mating, she wasn't sure, from the treetops and a warm, gentle wind blew over her as she waited. It really was a nice little clearing, she supposed. Much nicer than some of them she had spent time lying in wait for one beast or another.

At least it wasn't raining, she reassured herself.

Or worse, snowing. There wasn't much worse than having to remain still, waiting for a beast to appear, while being slowly covered in a layer of ice and snow. A small part of her was still amazed that she had survived the last time she had done precisely that.

It took the entire night and most of the next morning before there was any movement in the grass that was caused by neither the goat nor any of the smaller creatures that had come in to investigate. Without moving any more than absolutely necessary, Wendi turned her full attention to the movement, hoping that it was the goatsucker and not another, less desirable predator. The last thing she wanted to do was start all over again. The creature in the grass crept slowly and stealthily toward the goat and she strained to catch a glimpse of it.

The chupacabra was about three feet tall with leathery greenish-grey skin and a row of short but sharp-looking spikes running down its back. It moved slowly toward the goat, hopping carefully and silently, perfectly balanced on its hind legs. Now certain that this was the creature she had been waiting for, Wendi smiled to herself in equal parts relief and excitement and crept closer.

Even had she not been certain by visual inspection, the smell confirmed her identification as the odor of rank sulphur filled her nostrils and she had to swallow the urge to vomit. Slowly and carefully, she pulled a leather strap from her belt and felt for the other two straps to ensure they hadn't moved from where she had placed them. Each strap had a short length of chain attached to the end, made of light but sturdy rings. She balanced the straps in her hand, careful to keep the chains from alerting the creature to her presence.

The goat's bleating changed as it finally became aware of the predator that stalked it. From the low, argumentative grumbles that had echoed through the clearing since being placed there, its bleating became a cry of terror as it tried to escape its tether in earnest. Its thrashing did no good, however, as the iron spike kept it held securely in place.

The chupa hissed, a low trilling sound, as it hopped closer to its hapless victim. Its mouth opened to reveal long, sharp but hollow teeth. Spittle dripped from one fang to the ground below. It settled down on its haunches, preparing to spring into attack. Before it was able to sink its fangs into the goat, Wendi sprang from her hiding place and looped the thick leather strap around its neck, pulling the chain that held it in place as tightly as she could.

It screeched, turning away from its prey and toward her. She stepped backward quickly, knocking it off balance and pulling a second strap from her belt. This one went around the beast's long muzzle and she cinched it tightly before attaching it with well-practiced fingers to the chain she already held.

Powerful, talon-tipped legs kicked out toward her as the chupacabra scratched at its bonds with its tiny upper claws, trying to free itself. Wendi pulled another set of straps from her belt, this one a set of two straps that were connected in the middle, designed specifically for capturing one foot at a time.

Once she had the chupacabra as secure as she could possibly get it, she dragged it by the chains to her cart. Small as the creature was, chupacabras were vicious creatures and Wendi knew better than to try and carry it anywhere. There was a small winch attached to one of the wagon's crossbars and she attached an end of the chain to it, hauling the creature onto the wagon so she could get to work.

As the goatsucker's blood drained into the large barrel, Wendi went to fetch the goat. "Maybe I can get my money back for it," she thought hopefully to herself as she walked.

Or maybe she couldn't. The goat's bleating stopped abruptly as she approached, which she initially thought meant that the blasted thing had escaped, not a total loss in her opinion. However, she soon discovered that the goatsucker she had hauled into the wagon was apparently not the only one that roamed that particular field.

She smiled to herself and crept back to the wagon to grab another set of straps. The only thing better than getting a chupacabra was getting two of them. Her smile widened as she realized that, better yet, she wouldn't have to deal with the cursed goat anymore, either.

As the blood from the second goatsucker cascaded into another collection barrel, she tucked a hand into her pocket and her smile faded. She pulled out one of the pages she had ripped from the walls in town and looked down at the offensive words.

"Where is Basch?" she wondered. She had never even heard of the town. Considering how extensively she roamed the Inland Empire in search of goods to stock the shelves of her shop, for her to come across the name of a place with which she was unfamiliar was unusual indeed. Slave keeping was illegal in the Inland Empire and had been for some time. Despite her initial thoughts when she had first spotted the fliers, she knew that the residents of Landon hadn't been responsible for the posting of the pages. Whoever had placed the fliers had been brazen indeed to have risked arrest for such a ridiculous task.

When Wendi returned to Dragon Keep, Crucian was waiting at the entrance to the keep. "You've got a visitor," he explained once she was within earshot. "Waiting to see you inside." She looked past him toward the small, barely-used tavern but couldn't see to whom he was referring. Parked next to the tavern was a large wagon filled with enormous blocks of cut and shaped stone.

"Can't Phemie deal with them?" she asked, weariness evident in her voice. After all, that was the reason she'd left the witch in charge in the first place.

"Nope," he shook his head. "She said this was not to be her decision and to wait for you."

"Fine," she sighed. It was always frustrating to have people waiting for her when she arrived home. After a long night, the last thing she wanted was to deal with people. "Take the chupa blood inside," she instructed him. "I'll deal with our guests." She wasn't looking forward to it and she really hoped that her initial guess that the wagon belonged to a member of the stonemason's guild was wrong. She didn't need to buy any more stone; she had plenty of it crumbling all around her. What she needed was people to help her clear the stone and other rubble so she could start using some of the other buildings that were hidden under debris throughout the keep.

Without argument, Crucian took control of the heavy wagon, easily guiding it around to the narrow path leading behind the buildings. As soon as he was gone, Wendi headed upstairs to her small suite of rooms. Rather than the nice long bath that she would have loved to take, she settled for a change of clothes and a quick wipe-down to get as much of the road grime from her skin as she could.

Downstairs, feeling much better if not completely clean, Wendi headed for the small tavern, dismayed that it looked exactly the same as it had when she left. She had spent most of the last few months cleaning it out and polishing the wooden surfaces before moving in new furniture. That didn't even count the amount of time she had spent gathering wines, bitters, meads and ales with which to stock the bar. Eventually, she wanted to get some better spirits to serve as well but until then, what she had was what she had.

A couple of wandering adventuring groups were seated at the tables, drinking ales and telling tales that grew taller by the mug. "I'm telling you," one of them slurred, "it just swooped down, like that, and picked up the entire wagon, horses and all!" he gestured with his entire arm, mug in hand, as he demonstrated the maneuver. Ale sloshed onto the floor at his movements.

"Aw, come on," another member of his party argued. "Condorals don't get that big. The most a condoral could've snatched away would be a boot or two." A round of laughter spread through both adventuring groups at that and Wendi shook her head. The problem with the adventuring groups she had seen was that you couldn't believe a word any of them said. She just hoped they didn't make too big of a mess as they swapped their stories.

At a third table, a single woman sat, sipping patiently at her drink and ignoring the raucous crowd. She was tall and lean, perhaps not quite as tall as Wendi but nearly so. Her hair was long and thick, falling in golden waves to the top of her shoulders. A warm woolen cloak was wrapped around her shoulders, covering the long blue travelling robes she wore beneath.

"Analisse," Wendi greeted her with cheer. "How nice to see you again." Analisse had been a regular visitor to Dragon Keep since she and her Academy friends had discovered that they could get their components in Wendi's shop instead of hunting all over the Inland Empire to find them. Her influence had been directly responsible for the initial success of Dragon Trading. "What brings you here today?" Though she didn't see the younger woman nearly as often, now that she had finished her studies at the Academy, Wendi still considered the mage to be a friend.

"Business," Analisse replied as she set her drink on the table and turned to face Wendi, a glint of amusement in her eye. "Business that can help both you and us."

"Us?" Wendi raised an eyebrow as she sat across from the younger girl. "Do I get to know who 'us' is?"

Analisse chuckled. "My friends Remy and Phalant," she explained. "We were all students together at the Academy."

"I think I remember them." Actually, she knew she remembered them. Remy had been a small but boisterous young man, always cracking jokes and making small illusions to startle people. Phalant, quite the opposite, was tall and stoic. As far as Wendi had seen, Phalant had been much more serious than his friends, rarely talking but when he did speak his mind, his words had been wise. "What business are you thinking?"

"Well," Analisse began, "I'm not sure if you know this but during my studies, I was specializing in planar travel. Remy and Phalant are both enchanters." Although Wendi had never been specifically informed what each of their areas of focus had been, it had been easy enough to guess from their purchases. "Among all of us, we came up with an amazing new creation." She grinned excitedly, pride beaming out of every pore.

"One of the primary things I was studying was the portal system and..." she paused for effect, "I think I've figured out how they work." Portals were large golden spheres which had been placed in strategic locations around the Inland and surrounding Empires. With a single gold tyro, a person could travel instantly from one portal to any other portal to which it was connected.

"Ours –we're calling them transport gates, just so there's no confusion between ours and the existing portals - are smaller," Analisse continued, "But they cost a lot less to make. We plan to put a lot of them in service, a whole network of them, so that even the smaller towns that don't have portals can benefit from the ability to travel faster and further than they can over land or by sea."

Her argument made a lot of sense. Travelling by road was dangerous with bandits and thieves hiding behind every bush and travel by sea was even worse. The single connecting channel between the Inland Sea and the larger Azul Sea was known as the Pirate Run for a reason. With Analisse's new gate network, if it was as effective as she seemed to believe it was, traders and merchants wouldn't have to put their lives, or their livelihoods, on the line every time they went out to do business.

"So how much are you planning on charging for these transport gates?" While Wendi thought the idea sounded marvelous, she wasn't sure she would be able to afford being added to Analisse's new transport gate network. At the very least, the question would let her know how much she would have to save up in order to purchase one, after she confirmed how well they worked, at the very least. She wasn't in the business of making large purchases without first understanding what she would be getting for her coin.

"Nothing." Wendi looked at her doubtfully but Analisse was quick to clarify. "We're not charging for the gates. We'll install them for free but we take forty percent of all the passage fees."

This idea didn't make much sense to Wendi. "Why are you not charging to install the gates?" If they worked as well as she appeared to believe they did, she could get a decent price for each installation.

"We may later," the mage admitted, "but we don't expect many people to give us large sums of money on our word alone. We decided it would be best if we set up at least a portion of the network at our own expense first to get people familiar with the gates and how they work. Once people are used to using the gates, we expect people to start requesting them and we will start charging at that point."

Her explanation had merit. "And how much are passage fees?"

"One sheckle per person per direction." Silver sheckles were worth only a tenth of a tyro, so Analisse and her partners wouldn't be making much money from each individual passage, particularly since they would only be receiving forty percent of each silver coin. However, because of the smaller fee, they would likely see a lot more traffic passing through their gates, so that could make up at least some of the difference.

"You won't even have to place a fee collector at the gate," she explained further. "We include a collection box with the installation. All you'll have to do is collect your earnings at the end of the day. Our portion is transported directly to us."

She grinned again. "Plus, we'll give you one free transport charm. That will let you, or whoever you give it to, pass through any of our gates for free."

Wendi considered the idea while Analisse drank more of her wine. She didn't really have to consider it; she already knew it was a great idea. Having a gate would draw more business to her keep, plus it would offer her easy access to every other town in which a transport gate was placed. That could allow her to gather her materials and components a lot more quickly and easily than using her current method. The more the gate network expanded, she realized, the more benefit she could reap. Considering that Analisse and her business partners offered to install the gates for free so that there were no up-front costs involved, there was really nothing to lose.

"So, what exactly do I need to do in this?"

"We just need a patch of ground to put the gate in. At least a ten-foot square."

As soon as Analisse finished her drink, she followed Wendi out to the courtyard. Wendi pointed to a section of the yard, just inside the retaining wall and Analisse went to fetch her wagon. "It takes about a week to install everything," she explained. "Once it's up, you'll be free to travel the country."

3

For the first month after the transport gate was installed, Wendi was away from Dragon Keep more often than not. She travelled the Inland Empire, bouncing from gate to gate just to see how far she could go. Although the weather warmed steadily, she kept her cloak on and her hood up. The last thing she needed was to arrive in a town to which she hadn't yet been and cause a panic before even getting the chance to explore.

Three Rivers, with its soaring towers and the sleek grandeur of the Academy was, of course, equipped with a gate. It had a portal as well, Wendi knew, but the newest transportation device was on the opposite side of town from the portal. Whether that had been done to ensure continued movement through the existing portal or to allow those who couldn't afford the more expensive travel ease of access to the smaller transport gate, she wasn't sure.

It had been a long time since Wendi had been in Three Rivers and she didn't plan to stay long now that she was there again. The town, though large and welcoming, had never felt comfortable to her. As she walked down the wide, cobblestone-paved streets, she couldn't help but feel that there were many more eyes on her than just those on the road around her. Though she tried to shake the feeling away, deep inside, she realized that it was probably true. Mages littered the town like falling leaves in autumn and most of them had watching devices scattered all over the place.

Landor, the town she had been to only recently in search of a chupacabra had installed a gate as well. She started to wander the town, pleased to see that all of the offensive posters had at last been removed, until she heard the unmistakable sounds of hushed whispers and quiet conversations following her. Looking around, she spotted over a dozen people, hands to their mouths to cover their speech. Remembering how her hood had slipped the last time she had been there and not wanting to give the townspeople enough time to remember that they were supposed to be afraid of her, she slipped back into the gate quietly and headed to her next destination.

Wilee, on the southeastern shore of the Inland Sea, was her next destination on the transport gate network. Wendi was surprised to see that the small town even had a gate, as there was little of value to most people in the village. Apparently, Analisse had been serious about her stated intention of connecting as many of the small towns as she could with the gate network.

For her own reasons, Wendi was happy to see that there was a gate there. The Raknid Forest just south of Wilee was home to Stillok spiders, which were a breed of enormous spider whose venom she was constantly running short of. Now, with the gate in place, she would have a much easier time resupplying.

The next stop, however, excited her the most. As she stepped through the gate, she discovered that she was in a little town called Hoem, built directly on the edge of the Inland Sea. That town was where McClannahan Trading, the largest trading company in all of the Inland Empire, was based. As soon as she landed in Hoem, Wendi went immediately to speak with the owner of the trading company.

The offices of McClannahan Trading were located in a small set of warehouses just far enough away from the shoreline that they wouldn't be overwhelmed during one of the occasional storm surges that rampaged across the Inland Sea. There was a friendly young man humming to himself as he rummaged through a series of wooden crates that had been carefully stacked along the back wall. "Mr. McClannahan?" she asked tentatively.

"What?" The man looked. up, obviously startled. "Oh, you mean John. He's out on a run right now. Can I help you?"

Wendi introduced herself and explained that she was the proprie-tress of Dragon Keep. "We just got our gate," she explained helpfully.

"Hmm," he looked at her thoughtfully. "Like I said, John's out on a run and I'm not sure if he's looking to expand right now or not. But I'll let him know you stopped in if you want to leave him a message." He moved cautiously toward her, holding out a piece of paper and a quill. Most people weren't sure what to make of Wendi when they first met her so she wasn't taken aback by his reaction. The fact that she never lifted her hood so he couldn't get a good look at her face was unsettling, she knew, but it was much less unsettling than it would have been had she shown her face to him.

She jotted a quick letter of introduction and left it with the young man at the office. She wasn't sure whether she expected John McClan-nahan to open trading with her or not but it was worth the try. After all, if the adage that you only get what you ask for was true, then she couldn't complain if she had never asked.

There were a couple of other towns closer to the Pirate Run that had transport gates but, after some consideration, Wendi decided not to go to any of them. Although she had no quarrel with pirates personally, she also had no interest in actively requesting trade with them.

Most of the towns she had been to so far had been places she had visited at one point or another over the previous five years. They changed slowly, so there wasn't much reason to explore them thor-oughly because she had already done so recently enough to feel secure in what she would find. Instead, she wanted to see somewhere new, somewhere she hadn't yet seen and would, hopefully, offer exotic goods for sale that she could bring back home and put on her shelves.

The next gate to the south was a small fishing village called Clark-ton. When she stepped through the gate, she discovered that she must have travelled a decent distance after all because the air was substan-tially warmer and more humid there than it had been in Hoem. In fact, though spring had only just begun, it felt like high summer was already in full bloom. She quickly heated under her cloak but kept it in place regardless.

Clarkton seemed to carry mostly textiles. Wool and cotton fabrics were everywhere and many of them had been dyed in fantastically bright colors. Cotton and wool weren't exotic enough for her tastes, pretty as they may be, so she continued to travel south. She did, however, make a mental note to let Phemie know about the textiles there, as the witch was always looking for new fabrics with which to expand her wardrobe.

Dive was even hotter than Clarkton but it didn't matter. All of Wendi's discomfort disappeared as soon as she stepped into a shop and discovered that it carried live sea urchins. She eagerly purchased a dozen of the small, spine-covered creatures and the skin, cleaned and tanned, of an entire shark. She also picked up an assortment of shark-meat steaks, thinking they would be a welcome treat for her friends back home. Almost as an afterthought, she selected a small assortment of smoked fish to try.

Although her goods were packaged for travel, Wendi didn't want the meat to go bad or the urchins to perish so she went directly back home. In her absence, business had picked up but only slightly. There wasn't enough of an increase to warrant another trip out to gather more supplies, so Wendi handed the urchins over to Phemie, who squealed gleefully to see them. "I haven't had urchin in ages!" the witch exclaimed. "Can we have these tonight?"

"Not tonight," Wendi answered. "I've got shark steaks for tonight's meal." Phemie looked equally disappointed and excited at the meats Wendi had brought. Although Dragon Keep was next to a small river, few fish travelled far enough upstream for them to enjoy frequently.

The steaks were handed off to Crucian for grilling. She would have given them to Jaegar but he preferred his meat raw and had a difficult time understanding why other people wanted to cook their food, let alone how the process of doing so worked.

Wendi stayed in the keep for a week, waiting to see if any of her travels had brought more merchants to her shop but there were none so far. Disappointed but eager to explore further, she headed back to the gate. There were only three transport gates placed further south than Dive, so she wore her lightest-weight cloak to mitigate at least some of the stifling heat that she knew would be in store for her.

Ankh-Ra, on the northernmost edge of the Fusite Desert, was one of the most beautiful places Wendi had ever seen. The walls of almost every building in town were made from sandstone and they glittered and sparkled in the bright sun. The roads were paved with stones, smoothed from travel and regularly maintained. Near the gate, one of the first buildings she passed was the community bath, where men and women gathered to socialize.

As appealing as a cool, cleansing bath sounded, Wendi had no intention of disrobing in the company of strangers. Maybe, she thought to herself, if she ever manages to have both the time and the funds to do so, she could set up a personal bath similar to the ones in Ankh-Ra at Dragon Keep. How wonderful it would be, she thought as she wandered further down the street, if she could take a deep relaxing bath under the sunlight in the privacy of her own home. She was sure that Phemie would love to use it as well, but she had some small amount of concern about Jaegar and Crucian. While she wasn't opposed to letting them use her bath, they had made a substantial mess of the one she currently possessed the last time they had used it and had been banned from her chambers ever since.

She wandered from storefront to storefront, examining the available wares. She bought glass, baked from the desert sand and a large quantity of delicate sand rosettes.

"These sand rosettes," the helpful shopkeeper explained, "are collected before the rainy season hits every year." He explained how they formed when clumps of sand naturally adhere to themselves and were scoured by the surrounding sand, creating beautiful floral-shaped designs. Most of the sand rosettes Wendi had seen up to that point had either been very small or were cracked and chipped from transporting them but the ones she found in Ankh-Ra were palm-sized or larger and in pristine condition.

"Be careful you don't get these wet," he cautioned her. "They'll melt in water and turn back into sand."

She told a handful of the shopkeepers about her own store in Dragon Keep. She didn't really expect any of them to travel all the way to the Inland Empire to come see it, though it was much more readily available due to the placement of the gate network, but she figured that she was there anyway, so she might as well tell people about it.

Besides, she thought to herself as she headed back to the gate, *maybe one or two of them are curious about us up north, too.* She knew there were plenty of people who were curious enough about the southern lands and people.

Kowleun was every bit as beautiful as Ankh-Ra had been but the inhabitants were even stranger looking than those in the last town had been. The men all wore white or light-colored robes that covered them from shoulder to toe and matching light-colored cloths covered the tops of their heads and their hair.

The women were even more strangely dressed, with brightly colored but sheer fabric covering them from waist to ankle, with only a strip of matching cloth covering their most private areas from prying eyes. Embroidered and jewel-studded tops, again sheer around the arms, covered their upper bodies and most of them wore scarves across their faces that covered them from the nose down. Wendi watched in awe as green, blue, magenta and burgundy-clad women passed before her.

Although she knew that she would never wear it, she bought a pair of the sheer outfits for herself, one in magenta and another in a vibrant, cheery yellow. The face scarves would do nothing to cover her eyes but she loved the look and feel of the gorgeous fabrics. If someday she managed to find a way to change her eyes back to normal, she could wear the veil to cover her scar.

There were a handful of goods that she purchased for the shop as well but she was eager to head further south and see what kinds of glorious discoveries she could make. If the next town was anywhere near as exciting and exhilarating as the last two had been, she was in for a wonderful trip, indeed.

4

Basch was nowhere near as exciting or as marvelous as either Kowleun or Ankh-Ra. South of the desert that made the previous two towns shining oases, Wendi now found herself in a small city that could easily have been located within the Inland Empire. Or so she thought, until she headed further into the town and discovered a feature that would never have been found in her homeland.

In a roughly circular pen in the town square, men and women huddled while people outside the enclosure peered through the slats at the frightened captives and placed offers.

"Debtors," an elderly man with a thick cigar answered Wendi's question. "When you rack up a bunch of debt that you can't pay, you get sold to work it off." He continued to explain that this was the pen where those who had accrued a substantial amount of debt to either the town or to a particular person or establishment were held until someone paid their debts and claimed them.

"So as soon as their debts are paid off, they can go free?"

"Yep," the cigar-smoking man answered without bothering to look at her. "The purchase price is however much they owe. That debt is paid by whoever buys 'em and they can work their money back out of 'em however they want to."

Wendi looked into the pen, horrified. Some of the people looked like criminals but most of them looked just like normal people. "And anyone can buy them?"

"So long as they've got the tyros," he confirmed. "But we're about to close for the night. Come back tomorrow and you can pick yours then."

As she turned to leave, she spotted three more people. These weren't inside the pen with the rest of the debtors but were instead locked in stocks next to it. All three were bent over at the waist with their heads and hands trapped between thick slabs of wood. "What about those?" she asked. "Are they for sale too?"

"Yep," the slavemaster grunted. "But you don't want those ones."

"Why not?"

"Troublemakers," he answered. "That's what those ones are. Got themselves arrested after picking a fight in the tavern. Caused a lot of damage, that they did."

As he turned to walk away from the pen, Wendi called out after him. "Aren't they going to go back in the pen, too?"

"At sundown," he called over his shoulder. "They'll stay in the stocks until the sun's down."

Wendi stared after him, frustrated. She didn't like the idea of people being sold like livestock and she liked even less that some of them were locked in the hideous wooden contraption. There was no point in trying to call the slavemaster back, however, and she couldn't simply free any of the slaves. A group of five guards were stationed around the pen, most likely to prevent just such an occurrence. Two of the guards were stationed near the stockaded men and she wondered whether they were there to release the trio or to make sure they didn't manage to escape in the darkness.

Wendi went to the inn and got a room for the night. It was situated near the town square and her room had a window that looked down over the slave pen. As the sun dropped lower in the sky, she watched for someone to free the three men from the stocks but none came. Well after the sun had gone down and the rest of the town was asleep, the trio stood, bound in the heavy wooden device. Wendi could have screamed in frustration at how poorly they were being treated.

And, according to the slavemaster, it was over a stupid bar fight.

She counted the coins she had left, wishing she knew how much the prices on any of the slaves' heads were. There wasn't nearly enough, she knew, to buy freedom for more than just a handful of them. She wished she had brought more tyros with her. She debated on taking the gate back home and coming back with more money but she knew that it would be pointless. The town obviously thrived on its slave sales, so adding more to their coffers would only encourage more slavery. The practice was as disgusting to her as it was rewarding for those who partook in it.

In the morning, she watched for the slavemaster to arrive. As soon as she saw him walking up the street, she headed down the narrow flight of stairs and into the market. The man walked to the pen and counted the men and women left inside it before stepping over to the stocks. He said something that she couldn't hear but there was movement in response from the three men locked within them. Pulling a fat wad of keys from his pocket and aided by the guards, he released each of them in turn and led them into the pen.

The first one was tall and broad, with a chest almost wide enough to serve as a buffet table. He had thick muscle covering most of his body and there were a handful of scrapes and cuts covering his arms, likely from the fight they had been in and having been locked in the stocks overnight, in equal measure. His hair was long and brown, hanging down over his face like a curtain. Through the gaps in his hair, she could see sideburns on either side of his wide face but the center was clean-shaven but for a day's growth of stubble.

The second man was lean, wiry, and his head was clean-shaven. He had high cheekbones and a thin nose but when he walked Wendi was reminded of the movement of a deadly cobra as it was poised and ready to strike, even with the muscle soreness he undoubtedly had as a result of the uncomfortable position in which he had spent the night. His eyes were bloodshot but she could see that they were bright blue and constantly moving as he watched everything that happened around him.

The third one was not quite as tall as the heavily muscled man, with a fighter's build and an arrogant walk. He didn't step, he didn't shuffle his feet, he somehow managed to strut even while he was in chains. His hair was a deep orangey-red and when his glare turned in her direction, she saw deep brown eyes.

Once the slavemaster was seated on his little stool next to the pen's gate, she checked to make sure her hood was in place before approaching him. "Are you open now?"

"Yep," he answered as he lit the fresh cigar. Wendi wondered how many of them he went through in a day and how many of them were paid for by profits from the humans he sold like cattle. Blue-gray smoke gathered around him as he puffed.

"How much for that one?" she indicated an elderly man, stooped and graying with age.

"Three sheckles," he answered with barely a glance.

Three sheckles? Someone's grandfather was being sold as a slave over a meager three sheckles? As her ire grew, she tried to remain calm. "And that one?" She pointed to a young-looking woman who had spent most of the night crying.

"Seven sheckles."

"And what about the three that were in the stocks? You said they'd be for sale today."

"You don't want those, miss," he said, almost exactly as he had done the night before. "Those're dangerous."

"But they look strong," she improvised, wondering if her explanation would even matter. "I'm cleaning out my new keep and I need some people with strong backs to help with it." As far as she could tell, he was correct. All three of the men looked dangerous, particularly the lean one, but they looked more angry than violent. Considering that she intended to release them as soon as the purchase was complete, she doubted they would bring any harm to her.

The man sighed and puffed on his cigar for a long moment before relenting. "Two tyros for the small one." When she looked at him in surprise, he continued. "Another two and four sheckles for the big one." He looked into the pen and met the red-haired man's eyes. With a grin, he added, "And four tyros two sheckles for the other one."

She pulled nine tyros and six sheckles from her pocket and handed them over. It left her with only a little bit of money left but she felt that it was coin well spent. The slavemaster looked carefully at every coin, even biting each of the tyros to ensure they were genuine before gesturing to one of the guards to bring her purchases forth.

"Remember," he reminded her. "I told you those three were nothing but trouble." He grinned again. "And we don't give refunds."

"Fine," she snapped, thoroughly tired of the man's attitude. She was absolutely positive that she had been overcharged for the men but she didn't care. The slavemaster obviously had a grudge against them so the sooner she was able to get them out of his clutches, the better. Otherwise, she suspected, they would be resigned to the stocks again when night fell, just out of a perverse sense of amusement by the greedy little slavemaster.

The woman was brought out first, followed by the elderly man. Both of them walked over to stand docilely next to Wendi while the three younger men were brought out. All three of them glared at the slavemaster with undisguised hatred as they passed him but the seated man just grinned around his cigar.

"Now don't be like that, boys," he said. "We both know you'll be back in here with me soon enough."

The red-haired man clenched his fists at his words but to Wendi's relief he didn't punch the man. Not that she would have minded seeing the smug slavemaster lying unconscious on the ground but she wasn't sure she had enough money left to bail him out again.

She walked her small group a short distance away from the pen before speaking to any of them. "All of you are free to return to your homes," she said finally. "Your debts have been paid and I expect nothing from any of you in return." All five of them looked at her in astonishment but she waved them all away. "Go on. You're free."

"Bless you," the young woman said as she smiled gratefully at Wendi. "If there is ever anything I can do to repay you, please don't hesitate to ask." The old man had similar comments but Wendi waved him off as well. As she went to walk away, however, she realized that the remaining three men were still standing exactly where she had left them.

"Well?" she asked. "You're free. Go on home."

The one that reminded her of a cobra stepped forward, his head hanging low sheepishly. "We don't actually live here," he explained. "And we have no money to get where we came from." He looked at her, his eyes hopeful as he explained that all of their possessions were confiscated when they were arrested. "Is there any way we could work for you in some fashion? Just long enough to make enough money for us to get back home."

Wendi looked at the three men with dread. *How did that saying go?* she asked herself. *Something about how no good deed goes unpunished.* She didn't want the three of them hanging around but she couldn't just leave them stranded there. The vile little slavemaster would have them back in the pen before nightfall, of that, she was positive.

Or worse, she realized, he would have them back in the stocks.

Finally, she sighed. "Fine," she agreed. "Where's home?"

"In the Inland Empire," he supplied. "A little town on the Inland Sea called Hoem."

"But if we can get up to Dive or Clarkton," the big one added, "we can make it from there. His uncle," he jerked a thumb at the red-haired man, "owns a trading boat that stops there and his grandfather," he pointed at the snakelike man, "works on the boat, too."

Wendi nodded slowly. Of course, they would be from the Inland Empire. She had only travelled to almost the southern edge of the continent and into a completely different empire, so it made perfect sense that they would practically be her neighbors. "I could use some help carrying my purchases," she explained with a sigh. "You guys follow me and lift the heavy stuff and in return I'll take you all back to Hoem as soon as we're done."

The three of them blinked at her in surprise. "That's a long way away," the large one pointed out, as though she didn't already know. "We were just thinking we needed enough coin to board a ship or something."

"It's not as far away as you might think," she explained. "Hoem has a gate, just like the one here and the one at my keep.

"You guys can be back where you belong tonight."

5

The next afternoon found Wendi locked in her workshop with some of her newly purchased ingredients, absently chewing on a stick of licorice she had purchased the night before from a candy wagon in Hoem when she had delivered the men to their home. Her lab, as she called it, was in the basement of the main building of Dragon Keep, where the sturdy stone walls, floor, and ceiling would contain any explosions she might set off during her experimentations. A black scorch mark in the wall behind her worktable showed exactly how likely such an explosion could be.

And that had only been a small one.

"You have visitors," Phemie knocked as she entered. "Are you busy?"

While Wendi spent quite a lot of her time out gathering materials for sale in the shop, at heart she was an alchemist. Her lab was lined with shelves that were filled to overflowing with chemicals, venoms, toxins, fungi, and other bits and pieces that struck her fancy. However, some of her experiments could be delicate and required careful monitoring. Otherwise, she ended up with more scorch marks on her walls and ruined materials.

"Can you hold them off for a half hour or so?" she asked her friend without looking up from the calmly bubbling vial. As long as the bubbles stayed as they were, everything would be fine. If they turned to foam, however, she had a problem on her hands.

"No problem," Phemie sniffed at the air and wrinkled her nose. "What's in that?"

"Distilled cobra venom," Wendi replied calmly. She had found the substance in a seedy shop in Ankh-Ra. "I'm planning on adding it to a bottle or two of wine." If it worked out the way she hoped, she may have to pick up a live snake at some point in the future to keep a ready supply of the venom on hand.

"Why do you want to kill off your customers?"

"I don't." She pulled the half-chewed piece of candy from her mouth and looked over at her friend. "Distilling removes most of the toxin. It should just give the wine a little bit of a bite."

"Well," Phemie wrinkled her nose again, "just make sure we have plenty of the antivenin available before you start handing out samples." When Wendi just grinned at her and stuck the licorice back in her mouth, Phemie grumbled and closed the door behind her.

When Wendi made it upstairs, almost an hour later, Jaegar pointed her to a table in the tavern where three people were waiting for her. She handed him a bottle of wine. "Give this to Crucian, would you? And be careful not to break this one." As Jaegar shambled off, cradling the bottle in his arms as though it was a newborn child, Wendi turned to face her visitors.

An elderly but spry-looking man, a plump middle-aged woman, and an auburn-haired older gentleman were sitting at the table, waiting calmly for her arrival. Wendi stopped in surprise as she recognized the auburn-haired one as Bart McClannahan, mayor of Hoem. "Sorry to keep you waiting," she apologized as she regained her composure and stepped closer to them. "I trust you have been enjoying the hospitality." She stopped at the table and pulled out a chair to sit with them.

What is the mayor of Hoem doing in my tavern? she wondered. *And who are the other people?*

"How can I help you?"

The elderly man spoke for the group, to Wendi's surprise. She had addressed her question to the mayor, assuming that he would be the spokesman. Apparently, she had been wrong. She immediately turned her attention to the speaker. "We're here because of our sons. Or, in my case, grandson. I believe you met them yesterday. My name is

Wenson Bennett but everyone calls me Cookie. These are Kay Flingo and Bart McClannahan." Wendi nodded politely to each of them in turn, waiting to see what they wanted. "My grandson Oree, Kay's son Hannibal, and Bart's son Sean were the boys you returned to Hoem yesterday evening."

Great, she grumbled to herself. It had been annoying enough having to deal with the three men for most of the day before, now it appeared that she was going to have to deal with their families, too. "Is there a problem?" she asked, hoping that whatever the trouble was, she could get it taken care of quickly. She should have known that the red-haired man had been a McClannahan; he had the notorious family hair.

"We want to know how much you paid for the release of our children," Kay spoke up. "We appreciate your generosity and would like to be able to repay the money it cost you."

"No, thank you," Wendi replied. "I didn't do it with the expectation of being repaid. I just don't like slavery and the way they were being treated was shameful." When Cookie tried to protest, she held up a hand. "I don't want your money."

Mayor McClannahan seemed satisfied enough but Wendi's hope that they would leave gracefully withered as Kay took him by an elbow and settled him back down in his seat. "We simply cannot have you put out by our boys like that," she said, throwing a glare that could wilt bushes at him. "I think it would be best if we sent the boys back here to work off their debt to you."

"That is an absolutely marvelous idea," Cookie chimed in without giving Wendi a chance to protest. "As it looks like you have a lot of work to be done around here, the boys can help you out and start taking some responsibility for their actions." The last remark was accompanied by a telling glance at the mayor, so it wasn't hard for Wendi to recognize that at least part of the red-haired young man's attitude had been caused by his father being mayor.

"Look, I don't think that..." Wendi knew that she had already lost the argument. Even Bart McClannahan was looking as though he agreed with Cookie and Kay.

"Then its settled. They'll be here first thing in the morning," Cookie said as the three of them stood to leave. "You go ahead and decide what you'll have them starting on." She watched from her seat as the three of them walked to the transport gate and headed back for Hoem.

"Crucian says he needs another bottle," Jaegar stepped next to Wendi once the visiting trio was out of earshot.

"Of course he does," she sighed. "Did he get sick?"

"Nope." He looked thoughtful, not difficult considering that thoughts in and of themselves were difficult for the ogre-turned-human. "He burped a lot, though."

"Close enough," she muttered as she pushed herself to her feet. Perhaps having a stock of antivenin on hand wasn't such a bad idea after all.

Just after breakfast the next morning, three familiar shapes came walking across the courtyard from the direction of the transport gate. All of them had cleaned and the big one had his hair pulled behind him in a thick braid. He smiled when he saw Wendi, raising one enormous hand in greeting. The center of his face was freshly shaved and even his sideburns had been trimmed. Compared to how he had appeared when they had first met, he looked practically presentable.

The slender one had shaved as well so that no hair showed on either his face or his head but for his eyebrows and lashes. He didn't smile, but his eyes stayed on her for longer than she was entirely comfortable with before wandering again.

The third man, the mayor's son, had his red hair pulled back as well, although his was not braided. He still wore the same scowl as he had in the pen, which only deepened when he spotted Wendi. Of the three, he looked the least pleased to be there. On that, at the very least, he and Wendi were in agreement.

All three of them were carrying overnight packs and the big man held a small, foil-covered package. As Wendi approached, he held the package out to her. "From my mother," he explained. "She's a baker and insisted we had to bring you some sweet rolls."

She accepted the package but didn't look inside it yet. Instead, she used it to gesture to a building next to the tavern. "That's going to be an inn," she explained. "You guys get to clean it out and make whatever repairs it needs. Once that's done, I'll have your next task for you." She turned to head back to her lab. "I suggest you start by cleaning out a room or two so that you have somewhere to sleep tonight."

It wasn't unreasonable, she knew. Even in the main building of the keep where she, Phemie, Jaegar and Crucian lived, there weren't any other inhabitable rooms. They had only cleaned out enough for themselves. As with everything else, the main building was still a work in progress. No matter where the new three would be staying, they would have to clean out rooms in which to stay, so it just made sense that they should start by cleaning their own rooms out of the inn.

Behind her, she could hear that the men stood where she left them for the space of three or four of her steps. "Come on," one of them said finally. She recognized the voice as belonging to the smallest one. "We might as well get started."

Another voice protested but it was quickly silenced. Sean, she thought. That was what the mayor's son's name was. Of the other two, she wasn't sure which was Oree and which was Hannibal but she supposed she would find out soon enough.

When she came back out a few hours later to pluck some fresh mint from Phemie's garden, she spotted the men through one of the windows of the soon-to-be-inn. Hannibal and Oree were hard at work, removing debris and creating a large pile of trash to be removed on the side of the building. Sean, on the other hand, was perched sideways in the window sill, leaning against the stones on one side with his legs stretched out in front of him. As far as she could tell, the man was fast asleep.

Wendi said nothing to the men. Instead, she focused on quietly gathering her herbs and heading back down to her laboratory with them. If her erstwhile employee didn't want to work, she had no intention of forcing the issue.

When suppertime arrived, she went out to call everyone to the table. Since they didn't have a dining hall in the main building yet, she brought them to the tavern to eat where she had Crucian bring over plates of food, piled high, for each of them. Men that big, she suspected, would eat a lot. Particularly when they had been working all day. She personally followed Crucian with a pair of tankards, each of which was filled with Greystone mead. She set one down in front of the big man and one in front of the small one before taking her own plate and heading for her lab.

"Hey!" Sean called after her. "Don't I get some mead too?" The tone of his voice sounded as though he expected that the oversight had been nothing more than an accident, an impression Wendi was perfectly willing to correct.

"I gave you food," she explained coldly over her shoulder. "I gave you a warm place to sleep and the ability to honor your families' wishes by repaying your debt to me, despite my own reservations.

"Perhaps you should take a lesson from your friends. They worked today and by doing so earned their drinks. As far as I, or anyone else, saw, you did nothing but sit and whine all day." She stepped out of the tavern and walked across the quiet courtyard.

One of these days, she hoped, the courtyard would be filled with merchants, eager to buy her goods. Until then, she would just have to be patient. She tugged her hood lower over her face and continued walking.

6

Slowly, far too slowly for Wendi's taste but enough to notice, business was beginning to increase. As more people grew used to the transport gate network and more gates were activated, traders, merchants and curious townspeople came to check out Dragon Keep. Some of them just looked around the courtyard at the crumbling buildings and sparse amenities before turning around and leaving again but others actually came inside to do business. Some of the visitors bought goods and some sold. In a few cases, they did both.

A week after the men from Hoem arrived, Wendi came up from her lab and discovered that Phemie had placed a chalkboard near the shop's counter. The board announced that the shop now had attraction philters available for sale. The witch grinned at her as she read the sign quizzically.

"Attraction philters? You know how dangerous those can be."

"But everybody loves them," the witch protested. "After all, everyone wants to find love."

Attraction philters were short-duration spells that caused intense attraction from one specific person to one specific person. Wendi still shuddered at the memory of what had happened when Phemie had tricked her into handing one to Jaegar. She had needed to hide in her lab, the only room of the keep that he couldn't get into, in order to escape his overly-amorous attention. Thankfully, the philters only lasted for about a day, so once the spell wore off, he completely forgot about his infatuation with Wendi. A couple of their customers had been unhappy that the effect was so short-lived but Phemie's reaction was always the same: "What a difference a day can make!"

"It's not real love," Wendi reminded her. "It's a temporary thing."

It wasn't the first time she and Phemie had held that particular debate. Phemie was a staunch supporter of all things romance, despite her own lack thereof, so many of her potions were geared towards the consumer's love life. Despite Wendi's objections, however, people still came in regularly to purchase attraction philters from her. If absolutely nothing else, the witch understood their customers' desires.

"Great idea, isn't it?" Phemie said, interrupting her reminiscence. "It was actually Oree's suggestion. His grandfather has a restaurant in Hoem. He puts the daily specials on a board like this and it makes the sales of the advertised special increase by a lot." Oree was the smallest of the three men, Wendi had learned. The biggest one was Hannibal and she tried not to think about how much fun it must have been to give birth to a person that large. Although he had certainly grown some since then, she couldn't imagine that he had been a small baby.

"What have you got there?" Apparently noticing for the first time that her friend was carrying new items, Phemie came closer to investigate.

Wendi set a small box on the counter. "These are chewing gum samples," she explained. "They're for the customers, so don't let Crucian and Jaegar eat all of them."

Phemie reached for one of the small sticks inside the box. Half of them were wrapped in blue waxed paper and half in red. "What's so exciting about chewing gum?" she asked, looking at a blue-wrapped piece doubtfully.

To demonstrate, Wendi picked up a piece wrapped in red paper. She popped the gum into her mouth and softened it by chewing. "First of all, they taste good," she explained with a smile. "But if anyone wants to blow bubbles with it, they need to go outside and face away from the building." She did so as she spoke, taking three steps from the door. Not only Phemie but the handful of traders who had been perusing the shelves followed her outside, curious to see what was about to happen.

Smiling again, she turned to face away from the building but still where her audience could see what she was doing. She blew a bubble with the gum, stretching it until it was almost the size of her face until the bubble thinned enough to split open. As it popped, a small fireball shot a few feet out from the bursting gum before fizzling.

It had taken most of the last couple days for her to get the recipe right. Now, she was happy with it and Crucian's face had grown back from her last failure. Even though the fireball had ignited in his mouth, he had immediately shoved in another piece.

Wendi would never understand that guy.

"The red-wrapped ones are cinnamon fire," she said as she turned back to her friend. "The blue ones are summermint lightning."

"You gonna show us what that one does too?" A voice called out from the gathered merchants.

"Sure," she agreed amicably. "But not right now." While the amount of gum diminished with every fireball, there was enough in each stick for about five bubbles in her best estimation. "Once you take it out, though, it doesn't work anymore."

Back in her lab again after the demonstration, Wendi flipped through her notes, growing more frustrated with every page she turned. Creating the chewing gum had been fun but it was only a distraction. Eventually, she knew, she would find something that would allow her to look like a normal person again. She slammed a stack of papers down and pulled another stack off of her cabinet shelf. There were two cabinets in her lab, both of which she kept locked when she wasn't actively using the contents stored within them. The first held her most expensive and rare, not to mention dangerous, ingredients. The other cabinet, which was currently open, held all of her research and notes.

The scar was something she could deal with. As ugly as it was, it didn't bother her overly much. Sure, it itched occasionally but at least it didn't hurt. But she would give just about anything to have normal-looking eyes. The rest of her could stay exactly as it was and she wouldn't care so long as she didn't have to wear the cursed hood every time she was out in public. It was humiliating, pure and simple. Phemie had once pointed out that the hood made her appear mysterious but Wendi knew that her friend had just been being kind.

"Why do they have to look like that?" she questioned aloud. She often spoke to herself while in her lab, so anyone passing by was unlikely to think much of it. "I've never even heard of this happening to someone else, so why did it happen to me? And how did it happen?"

She looked like a freak, and she knew it. She couldn't stand the way people looked at her with the hood as though she was a curiosity, some strange fool who refused to show her face. Even that was better, however, than the looks she got when she didn't have the hood. People called her a monster, they called her a demon. As she looked at her reflection, she couldn't help but understand why they thought that way.

Human beings have a wide range of colors to their eyes. They have cool blues, warm browns, watery greens, even the occasional silvery-grey or fascinating violet. Most often, eyes contained many different colors, but one thing all of them had was white. Around the circle that held the color, the human eye was white. Although there were more variations in them, even most of the wild animals that could be encountered had white in their eyes as well.

Her eyes, on the other hand, were completely, utterly black. There was no color, there was no white. There was just a void where her soul was supposed to shine.

She flipped through more papers, unrolled more scrolls. The biggest problem, she knew, was that she had no idea what she was supposed to look like. "Am I supposed to have brown eyes or blue? Were they supposed to be silvery grey, or were they that fascinating shade of hazel that looks gold?" If only she knew, she might have an idea of how to change them back.

She had also spent no small amount of time wondering whether her hair was supposed to be black, or whether that was caused by a similar effect to what had happened to her eyes. So far, she'd been able to come up with a way of changing her hair color but the color always grew out. There wasn't any way that she had found of permanently changing it so that new hair grew out in the desired color. Hair color, like eye color, was made of thousands of smaller colors all mixed together to create an overall effect. Did she have blond hair or brown? Or perhaps red, like Sean's. She had no clue. She sighed and dropped the scroll, reaching for another.

She had found ways of growing taller and shorter, not that either of them mattered. None of her friends knew what she was truly looking for. Except Phemie, perhaps. Wendi suspected that Phemie had an idea about what so many of her experiments had been focused on. Thankfully, the witch had never asked her about it.

"Perhaps troll blood would help," she muttered as she opened yet another scroll. She reached over and put a mark on her chalkboard, a reminder to keep an ear out for troll activity. Since trolls were renowned for their regenerative ability, their blood was in high demand. Even if she didn't end up using it to find a solution to her own personal problem, it would be a good thing to have in stock.

Hopefully Crucian wouldn't mind.

With a growl of frustration, she threw all of her notes back into the cabinet and locked it. She was supposed to be working on developing a salve that she had been trying, off and on, for over two months to get right. It was a mixture of many different pain-relieving herbs, many of which she had used on a regular basis to relieve the pain in her face. She wanted to make it potent enough to numb an injury but not so potent that it killed all sensation permanently.

If she could get it right, she figured that it would be handy to sell to adventurers. They were always heading out in an attempt to get themselves killed – sometimes successfully, sometimes less so. Physicians might be interested in it too. They were frequently called on to treat the aforementioned adventurers, not to mention the regular townspeople who receive grievous injuries through their normal daily living.

"Might even be useful to keep some on hand here, too," she mused to herself. If the men from Hoem got injured while working on her keep, she would have no option but to treat their wounds as best she could, treatment that would likely go a lot smoother if they weren't in pain from their injuries.

On her last wander, she had stumbled across an unusual fungus in a cave near Landor. It caused the numbness she was looking for but it also knocked whoever came too close to it unconscious. Gathering it had been an experience she wasn't eager to repeat. However, if her latest guess proved to be correct, it just might provide the critical ingredient to her salve to make it work correctly.

7

She continued to work on her salve for a week, brewing and discarding batch after batch of failed experimentation. Occasionally, she would come upstairs to check on the status of some of the other concoctions she made but she spent the vast majority of her time in the lab. Work on the inn was progressing steadily, despite the continued lack of effort from Sean. Oree and Hannibal seemed more than happy to put in a full day's work, however, so she was willing to overlook Sean's laziness.

Sean still didn't get mead, wine, or anything but water at mealtimes. He protested, of course, but Wendi had stopped bothering to explain to him that until she saw him actually working, he got nothing. She didn't particularly care what kind of special treatment he was used to receiving at home but, in her keep, he could expect none.

Traders were coming to Dragon Keep with more frequency, which she was more pleased to see. Some of them were new trading companies, just as eager to capitalize on the new gate network as Wendi herself was. Others, such as McClannahan Trading, were older, more established companies. All of their purchases had started out small but soon she was trading in larger and larger quantities of goods. Twice now, she had needed to put her research on hold so that she could go out and resupply.

When she came upstairs with a small jar of salve that she thought was ready for testing, she discovered that not only Sean but Oree and Hannibal were standing idly in the courtyard, ogling a pretty young merchant as she loaded fresh goods into her cart. Tugging her hood down lower over her face, she strode across the yard toward them. "Go home." She didn't bother explaining further, her statement had been succinct and clear. Even Sean should have no trouble understanding what she had meant.

However, as had happened on far too many occasions, her mouth decided that more words were necessary. "If you're not going to do anything while you're here, you can be elsewhere. I'm not running a child care center."

All three of them stared at her in surprise but she didn't care. She realized that her words were unfair to Oree and Hannibal, as they had been diligently working every other time she had come out to check on them. She really couldn't blame them for taking a break on occasion. She turned to head back in search of Crucian.

As she walked away, however, she heard Sean's voice quite clearly. "Getting out of this was even easier than I thought." She could hear the smirk in his voice and, before realizing what she was doing, she had turned back to face them.

As she had thought, Sean was grinning widely, obviously pleased with himself. The other two had been trying to shush him and Hannibal quickly stepped backward as Wendi faced them. "You want it easy?" she asked, letting her irritation at the entire situation shine in her voice. "Fine. Let's see how easy this can be for you." She had taken enough of Sean's snide comments and lousy attitude, particularly considering that she had never wanted any of them there in the first place.

"You are the sorriest excuse for a man I have ever seen. You are lazy, rude, obnoxious, and I can hardly stand the sight of you." Even Oree backed away beneath her quiet fury. "The only reason any of you are here is because your families wanted you to learn how to take care of your own problems but apparently you are simply incapable."

"Now you wait just a minute," Sean's grin was gone, faded into shocked disbelief. Wendi wondered if he was so surprised by her words because nobody had ever bothered to tell him what an obnoxious jerk he really was before. She suspected she was right. "You can't talk to me like that. I've spent weeks here, helping you put your little keep back together again."

He would have continued, but she interrupted him. "No, you haven't. Your friends have. You haven't managed to pick up even so much as a shovel. Are you afraid to get your pretty little hands dirty?"

She knew the moment her hood slipped, and she could have kicked herself for getting so worked up that she hadn't realized how far it had moved until it was too late.

Sean took a step backward, horror and disgust crossing his face as her eyes, unblocked by her hood, came into view. "What the hell are you?"

Rather than screaming in rage, she did what any rational, reasonable person in her position would have done.

She threw the bottle at him.

The delicate glass shattered as the bottle struck his chest and he gasped before falling to the ground, motionless. He was still breathing but it appeared that rather than numbing where it touched skin, the salve had deadened his senses everywhere. She frowned and nudged him with the toe of her boot but he didn't seem to react. His eyes, however, were alert and staring accusingly at her, so she calmly lifted her hood and replaced it over her face before turning to Hannibal and Oree.

"It'll wear off in a couple hours," she reassured them, her anger replaced with chagrin at her own behavior. "Take him home and don't bother coming back." She didn't watch to see as Hannibal and Oree lifted their stricken friend and carried him to the gate.

If nothing else, she reasoned with herself as she walked back down the steep stairs to her laboratory, she had discovered that the latest batch of salve was potent enough to work through clothing.

"Can I have one?" Crucian looked longingly at the bottles of snakewine as Wendi arranged them on a shelf in the tavern the following afternoon. "Just one?"

She opened her mouth to tell him no but as she turned to face her friend, she noticed three people walking across the courtyard. "What in the blazes are they doing here?" she grumbled irritably. She had only sent the Hoem trio away the day before and couldn't imagine what had brought them back to Dragon Keep so quickly. Again, Hannibal carried a small wrapped package of baked goods and Wendi's mouth watered at the sight. Although she hadn't told anyone, the sweet buns he had brought with him the last time they had arrived had been some of the best sweet rolls she had ever tasted.

"I told you to leave," she said coldly as they walked into the bar. "What part of 'don't come back' was confusing?"

"We weren't given a choice," Oree answered as they stopped in front of her. He looked embarrassed as he said it and even Hannibal managed to look sheepish. Sean, on the other hand, looked as defiant as always. "My gran said that there was no way we could have already paid back our debt to you and that we were to come back until it was clear."

Wendi could understand why their families had sent them back to her. Goodness knew how many other times they had gone out and gotten themselves in trouble and relied on their families, particularly the McClannahan family, to bail them out. Hannibal and Oree, at the very least, seemed to have some sense about them and she would be willing to let them come back and work. Sean, on the other hand, seemed to have no self-discipline whatsoever and appeared perfectly content to let his friends assume the lion's share of responsibility.

She stared at them for a long moment before answering. "No," she said simply. "I'm heading out of town this afternoon and I don't believe you three will do much of anything in my absence." She looked pointedly at Sean, who seemed to have recovered from the previous day's shock. Now, he just stood before her, thumbs tucked comfortably in his belt, and looked directly where her eyes would be, had they not been covered by her hood.

"Perhaps we can come with you," Hannibal offered. "The three of us have a lot of experience with travel and if anything comes up – such as bandits and the like – we may be able to assist you in that way."

His idea had merit, though Wendi was reluctant to admit it. She was heading out in search of a nest of gargoyles, violent, hideous creatures that existed only to kill out of a malevolent sense of glee. They posed a

real threat to many towns in the Inland Empire, partly due to their malevolent natures and partly due to the fact that they could hide in plain
sight, appearing as ordinary, inanimate statuary. Normally the danger
inherent in such creatures would be enough to dissuade her from
pursuing them but some parts of the gargoyle were in high demand for
magical components. As a result, she was constantly running low.

Wendi had no idea where the creatures had originated but she
suspected that they were magically created, which could also account
for their magical use. Similar beings ringed the roofs of large buildings, guiding rainfall away from the edge of the buildings. She had a
suspicion that living gargoyles had been created to be guardians of a
particular building, only to have the magical spells glitch somehow,
releasing the creatures from their magical bonds and allowing them to
spread and reproduce.

Worse, this nest was near the spider-ridden woods just outside
of Wilee. She had intended on bringing Crucian with her, as he was
immune to most of the spiders' poison, but due to the increased traffic
at the keep, Phemie may need his assistance while Wendi was gone.
Taking the three men in his stead seemed to be a reasonable tradeoff.

Hannibal continued to look pleadingly at her and she wondered exactly what kind of threat it had taken to get them to return to Dragon
Keep. After all, she had sent them home carrying Sean, who appeared
to have recovered nicely from the salve he had been splattered with.
She took a mental note of that fact. Knowing that the effects lasted for
less than a day was useful information.

"Besides," Oree added hopefully, "if we help you stock your shelves,
maybe that will pay down a little of what we owe you."

Plus, she realized as the scent of freshly-baked sweet rolls escaped
the foil-covered package and reached her nose, there was something to
be said about Hannibal's mother's form of bribery. Sean McClannahan
may have been a world-class pain in her backside but Kay Flingo's
baked goods almost made up for it.

Almost.

"Can any of you fight?" she asked facetiously. When Sean snorted in response, she looked levelly at him. "I'm going after gargoyles," she explained. "Those things are hard enough to take down without having to come in and rescue your sorry hides as well."

Sean began his lengthy explanation about exactly how phenomenal of a swordsman he was and Wendi waited patiently for him to finish.

"If you guys are so good," she wondered out loud once he finished bragging, "then how did you end up in the stocks in Basch?" She smiled sweetly, enjoying the expressions of shock on all three of their faces before turning to head back to the shop.

"I leave at dawn. If you guys plan to come with me, be ready by then." She took three steps away before turning back to the men. Soundlessly, she stepped over to Hannibal, took the wrapped package from his hands, and left them in the courtyard.

A girl's got to have priorities, after all.

8

Wendi couldn't decide whether she was pleased or dismayed when she found the trio waiting for her in the courtyard near the transport gate at sunrise the next morning. All three of them had packs slung over their backs and weapons strapped to their persons. Hannibal had an enormous claymore strapped to his back, a sword that was almost as long as he was tall and at least three hand's-breadths wide. Oree had a pair of shining steel swords, thin, light, and fast, clipped to his belt. Sean had a broadsword attached diagonally across his back, a long bow slung over one shoulder, and a small oval shield attached to one fore-arm. All in all, she had to admit that they looked ready for battle.

She just hoped they wouldn't get themselves, or her, killed.

"Everybody ready to go?" she asked as she guided her collection wagon toward them. "Last chance to change your minds."

"We're ready," Hannibal answered as he eyed the strange-looking wagon. "What's that for?"

"To put the gargoyles in, of course." She smiled at him as she moved the wagon next to them. "For now, just put your things in the back and hop in." All of them complied, wary but willing. As she headed for the gate again, she handed each of them a vial filled with pale green fluid. "There are woods where we are headed, filled with poisonous spiders. If any of you get bitten, you've got about a minute to drink this before the venom kills you." The anti-toxin was her own brew and she knew it worked. It had saved her life on more than a handful of occasions already.

"This looks like it probably tastes bad," Hannibal commented as he slipped the vial into a pocket.

"Very bad," Wendi agreed. "Better than the alternative, trust me." She headed for the gate, stopping to drop a coin in the collection box as she entered it. Though her medallion gave her free travel between gates, she had quickly discovered that it did not grant the same benefit to her cart or any passengers she carried with it. A silver sheckle was a small price to pay, however, particularly when six copper thalers of it would return to her own coffers that night.

Wilee was just beginning to wake as she and the men headed through town. There was nothing to draw her interest, so they headed straight down the road that led into the Raknid Woods. As they travelled deeper into the forest, Wendi kept a wary eye out for spider webs. The giant spiders that inhabited the woods grew as large as three feet across and before they had gone very far into the woods at all, she discovered their telltale webs. The webs stretched from tree to tree far overhead, thick, sticky strands of shimmering grey-white filament. Had she not been heading in search of more valuable prey, she might have been tempted to stop and collect some of it but since she didn't see any of the webs' creators, she pressed on.

"So how far out is this nest?" Oree asked while Wendi examined the treetops.

"About another hour or so," she replied. "There's a little village just off the Piedros River that they attacked just over a week ago. Most of the people fled but it's pretty safe to guess that the people who didn't make it out never will."

"I hadn't heard about that," Sean pointed out. "Where did everyone go?"

Wendi shrugged. "Other towns, I'd guess. I wouldn't be surprised if a few of them landed in Hoem." She spotted a spider moving through the webs overhead. Though it seemed to be moving in roughly the same direction as they were, it didn't seem to have noticed them yet. She looked back at the men, holding one finger to her lips to indicate that they needed to be quiet. When all of them looked at her question-ingly, she pointed up at the creature roving through the trees.

Natives of the Inland Empire and self-proclaimed explorers, none of them needed her to explain the need for silence. Stillok spiders were some of the deadliest natural predators of the woods around the Inland Sea. They thrived in the land that had plenty of game and though wild elk were some of their favorite foods, humans were a close second. Ever-present rumors circulated around the empire; stories of entire towns being swallowed by swarms of Stillok spiders during the dead of night. By the time morning came, the towns were coated in sticky webbing and nothing was left alive.

These rumors weren't just stories, as Wendi knew from personal experience. During her travels before meeting Phemie and setting up her shop at Dragon Keep, Wendi had come across one such spider-taken village. Though the spiders had moved on by the time she arrived, she would never forget the horror she had felt seeing the Stil-lok web covered buildings. Worse had been the husks of the spiders' victims, entombed in webs and drained where they had been overtaken in their beds.

Stillok venom wasn't just a regular toxin, either. It was acidic, so when the spider injected its poison into a victim, it began to dissolve it from the inside out. Only the dried, brittle skin and bones remained after the spider finished its meal.

There was one blessing, however. The spiders could neither see nor hear with any accuracy at all, so it was easy enough, if a traveler was careful, to pass by the deadly creatures unnoticed.

"I think we're clear," Wendi announced after seeing no sign of spiders for almost a mile. "The webs look like they're older out here, so I don't expect to see many more of them." Aside from the first spider she had noticed, five other spiders had been spotted during their journey through the wood. Now, as they entered a wide clearing that surrounded the village they had been looking for, she felt reasonably secure that they were safe from spider attack.

Gargoyles, on the other hand, could pose a whole new level of threat. She stopped the wagon at the entrance to the town where the wide wooden gates stood open, rendering the high stone wall that surrounded the town useless. As she looked inside, she was reminded once again of the silent, web-strewn village she had once explored.

Unlike the town from her memories, however, this one was completely devoid of webbing.

"I guess gargoyles don't like spiders invading their territory," Sean snickered and, for once, Wendi agreed with him. Given how long the village had been sitting empty, the spiders should have at least come closer to have a look.

"Everybody out," she said as the wagon stopped. "Be on your guard, though, and don't trust any statues you see."

"We know," Sean retorted irritably. "This isn't our first gargoyle, you know."

They headed cautiously into the town, watching along rooftops and beneath eaves, searching for any sign that a gargoyle was present. Moving as quietly as they could, they stepped further into the vacant village. Finally, Oree pointed ahead of them and whispered, "Found one."

Near the center of the town, a large carved stone fountain gurgled merrily as it spewed forth water from a handful of small copper pipes. On top of the fountain, a small grotesque statue sat patiently, water raining down over its head and wings and more rivulets ran down its body.

"Looks kind of small," Hannibal noticed. Most of the gargoyles Wendi had seen had been five to six feet in height but this one was less than half that. Its size wasn't the only indication of age, as this particular gargoyle hadn't yet grown its horns. Gargoyles were born with smooth, bat-like faces and heads but grew horns when they reached maturity. Given the shape of the small one's head, it was less than two years in age.

"Don't care," Sean grumbled. He unsheathed his sword and stepped closer, ready to attack.

"Wait," Wendi grabbed him by an arm and held him in place. While the men had been looking at the creature in the fountain, she had been scanning around the area looking for more of them. Where there were young, there were certain to be adults around. "That one's bait. Look." She pointed to the entrance of a building, not very far away from the fountain, where another pair of stone sentinels stood.

Sean's eyes narrowed, but he stopped moving. "Hannibal and I can take those two," he said quietly. "Oree, you get the one in the fountain." Both of the men nodded and unsheathed their weapons.

"Fine," Wendi agreed. "I'll take the three along the far wall."

All three of the men stared at her in shock at her announcement and Oree lifted a hand to shade his eyes from the sun's bright glare as he turned his attention to the back wall. "Change of plan." he swore quietly but emphatically. "Hannibal, you circle around and go for the gargoyles on the wall. Sean, you get the ones in front of the building. I'll take out the little guy and then back up Hannibal."

Wendi shook her head. Did they really think she had come unprepared? She pulled a large, bulky wooden contraption from beneath a canvas cloth and lifted it onto the cart's cage. As soon as she had it secured, she pulled a handful of enormous crossbow bolts from beneath the cloth as well. Snapping both of the device's arms out to the side, she locked the securing pins that would hold them in place. "How about I get the ones at the door and you three can fight over the rest?"

It wasn't much of a question. She plugged a small crank into the back of the device and began to twist it. A thick cable, stretching from the end of one arm to the other, pulled backwards slowly as she twisted the crank. When she had it back as far as she wanted it, she loaded the first bolt.

If there was one thing Wendi loved, it was the craftsmen at Greystone. They had designed and built the mobile ballista for her and every time she used it, she sent another word of thanks to its creators. She had a wide assortment of bolts for the enormous crossbow that were intended for an array of hazards but the ones she was using for the gargoyles had thin, strong mesh wire wrapped around the tip with weights scattered around the edges. When she reached down and pulled the release lever, the bolt shot straight and true, slamming into the first gargoyle.

It screeched as it was struck but she knew that it wasn't really hurt. Besides just looking like carved stone, gargoyles had exceptionally tough skin. It took a lot more effort to hurt one than just shooting a single bolt at it. When the projectile hit, the creature's thick hide stopped it from penetrating very far. The net that was attached to it, on the other hand, flung out in all directions, wrapping around the beast and effectively trapping it. Without use of its wings, there was no way for the creature to fly and it fell to the cobbled stones blow with a heavy thud.

"One down," she said calmly as she began twisting the crank again. "You guys might want to get a move on; it looks like the rest of 'em are waking up."

The second gargoyle that had been crouched in front of the building launched into the air, spreading out its leathery, stone-colored wings to gain altitude. Wendi calmly watched as it ascended, slipping another bolt into the ballista and waiting for it to come back into range.

"Watch the sky," Hannibal called out as the gargoyle rose. "They've got a nasty dive attack."

The creature in the fountain had taken to air as well, though not as high up as Wendi's target had. It swooped about thirty feet up before screaming and diving down at the three men who were running for all they were worth for the back wall. The three gargoyles that Wendi had spotted in that area spread their wings, preparing to take to the sky as well.

Oree stopped halfway across the courtyard, eyes cast to the sky to watch both of the airborne gargoyles, swords at the ready in his hands. Seeing a lone, unprotected target, the smallest creature headed directly for him. It screeched again, a sound that sounded more like triumph than anger, and reached its sharp talons to rake at him as it dove.

Moving as quickly as the cobra he resembled, Oree snapped his blades up to meet its attack. With one arching thrust, he trapped the small creature between his swords and used its own momentum to slam it down onto the ground. He pulled one of his swords back slightly before thrusting it into the creature, the thin blade finding one of the small, unprotected areas on the gargoyle's body. A second thrust with his other blade stilled the twitching creature.

He jumped backward, clearing almost four feet in distance, when the second mesh-tangled gargoyle fell to the ground. It wasn't close enough to have landed on him but it was more than close enough to have startled him.

Hannibal and Sean made quick work of their targets as well. By the time they came, panting from the exertion, back to the wagon, Wendi was halfway through the process of winching the first of her captured gargoyles into the back of her wagon. Oree's kill lay on the ground next to the wagon and he was snarling with effort as he pulled her second captive to join it.

"You guys want to bring yours over here too?" Wendi asked as the men drew closer. Her hood had fallen from her face during the battle and she hadn't bothered replacing it. They had already seen what she looked like beneath it and the gargoyles didn't care about her appearance.

Hannibal and Sean's shocked eyes traveled from her to the gargoyle she was hoisting into the wagon, then to the gargoyle that Oree was fighting to drag over. "You're serious," Sean sputtered. "You actually want to take them home with you?"

"Of course I'm serious," she answered as she secured the first creature into the wagon. "What did you think we were out here for, sightseeing?"

9

Phemie was ecstatic that Wendi had managed to bring back so many gargoyles and cackled the way that only a witch could as she carted the smallest carcass into her backroom workshop. "What are you going to do with the others?" she inquired as she walked past Wendi. "You're not planning to just release a pair of angry gargoyles out into the forest around here, were you?"

"Of course not," Wendi sighed. Her hood was back in its customary position over her eyes and she tilted her head as she looked at the interested people gathered around the wagon. Jaegar had already removed the dead gargoyles and it looked like he was trying to figure out what to do with the ones that were still moving.

"Should start a menagerie," Crucian offered. "People seem to like looking at 'em." He turned his doleful glance toward Wendi. "Maybe bring more here, too."

Wendi looked around doubtfully. "Interesting idea," she admitted, "but I'm not sure about having a bunch of dangerous creatures in my courtyard. If any of them get loose, a lot of people would end up dead."

"Cages," Crucian responded. "Big ones. Strong ones."

"Magically enchanted ones, perhaps," Phemie interjected. "I saw a travelling menagerie years ago that kept the animals in enchanted cages so they couldn't escape."

The idea had merit, she had to admit. Having some of these creatures nearby would make it much simpler to collect samples from them as she needed them and she had already intended on purchasing a cobra for just that reason the next time she was in Ankh-Ra. She had never considered the possibility that others might be interested in seeing some of the creatures she regularly dealt with as well. "How much do you think it will cost to get some of those enchanted cages?"

If they could set up a working menagerie, that could just be the additional draw to bring more people to Dragon Keep. If the attention the gargoyles were garnering was any indication, a lot of people would be interested in seeing the creatures up close and personally.

"I don't know," Phemie admitted, "but I'm sure I can find out. If nothing else, the Academy should have someone who can do it."

"Not sure I want to rely on a bunch of students for this," Wendi said cautiously. "If they don't do the enchantments right, that could give the animals a way to get out." She looked over at the live gargoyles that still struggled in the cart. "I think that would just cause a much bigger problem, don't you?" Much as she appreciated having a gargoyle nest close enough for her to travel to, she didn't relish the idea of having one in her own backyard.

Phemie agreed to check on expense for enchanted cages. She gave her word that the mages doing the enchantment would be fully trained, even if they were still students, which eased some of Wendi's concerns.

"For now," Wendi turned to Crucian, "Would you go help Jaegar? Put the live ones around back. I'll figure out what to do with them later." She picked up the assortment of gargoyle blood and skin that she had set aside for her own purposes and headed for her lab.

She had work to do. Restocking the shelves hadn't been the only reason she was so interested in getting her hands on some gargoyles.

Two days later, to Wendi's surprise, she discovered that the trio had managed to completely finish clearing out the inn. Hannibal took her inside to show her that all of the rooms were empty and, even more surprisingly, clean. "Phemie sent Oree down to the storage room," he explained. "He's getting furnishings for the rooms but we weren't sure what you wanted done with this room." He led her into a wide, open area that was surrounded with windows to let in plenty of light. "We were thinking it would work really well as some sort of a gathering area, a lounge for people to just sit and hang out, but we thought it'd be best to check with you."

She nodded, impressed. "You guys did a really good job in here," she smiled. "It looks great. And I think a gathering room is just fine for now. If I decide I want to change it later, I'll worry about it then." She looked around her new inn, pleased with the way it had turned out. The guys had managed to repair all of the damage, including the sagging rafter overhead that she had been worried about. Hannibal's sheer size had been beneficial in that repair, of that she was positive.

As she turned to leave, she asked, "You said Oree was getting furniture, right?" When he agreed, her smile faded. "Where's Sean?" From the expression on Hannibal's face, she immediately understood exactly who had been doing all the work, despite Sean's assurance that he would help. "Has he done anything in here?"

She found him exactly where she expected to find him, seated comfortably at a table in the tavern next door and drinking a glass of snakewine. Half the bottle was sitting on the table in front of him and she stopped in the doorway, staring at him in disbelief. Irritated, she stepped across the room to stand behind him, reached out and smacked him across the back of his head.

Her strike knocked him forward just as he was taking a drink, making him choke and cough on the spicy wine. To his credit, he managed to set the glass back onto the table instead of dropping it on the floor. He shot to his feet and spun to face her, still trying to breathe, his eyes almost as full of venom as his drink. "What in the hells was that for?"

"Your friends have been working their backsides off," she answered angrily. "They've cleaned out the inn and are even now moving new furniture into it. You, on the other hand, seem to have no skills whatsoever but for sitting on your lazy rump and drinking all my alcohol!"

"Now you wait just a minute," he argued as he took a step closer to her. "I was out there helping you with your precious gargoyles and you know it. There's no way you would have made it back alive if it hadn't been for me and my friends, so I think a little gratitude is in order."

"Gratitude?" She couldn't believe he had even suggested that she needed to be grateful to him. "I didn't ask you to come along with me to get the gargoyles, you guys insisted. I could have easily handled that myself. But as far as gratitude goes, how about a little gratitude for getting your sorry backside out of a slaver's pen?" she demanded. "Or have you already forgotten about that? If it wasn't for me, only the gods know how long you would have rotted in that filthy place.

"Unless, of course, you ended up in the stocks again."

"Yeah," he snorted. "It was so nice of you to save me from the slave pen like that. Heck, you're so nice you brought me all the way back up here to be a good little slave for you!" He reached down to pick up the glass once more. "Thought by now you'd have figured out that I'm nobody's slave."

"I told you to go home. Twice now, I have sent you home. The only reason you're here," she retorted, "is because your father sent you back here. I would have been perfectly happy to have never had to see you again."

"Surprised you can see anything out of those evil little eyes of yours," he sneered as he took another drink of wine.

Her hand collided with the side of his face before she had even realized it was moving. The force of the blow snapped his head to the side, stinging her hand and leaving an angry red welt across the side of his cheek where she had struck him. Glass shattered against the floor next to the table. "Get out," she screamed at him. "Go home and whine to your daddy about how awful your life has been; I'm sure he's already heard all of it.

"Go back and whine to your mommy like the spoiled little brat you are. Maybe, if you're really lucky, she'll give you a cookie to make it all better."

Furious and mortified, amazed that anyone had managed to make her so enraged, she spun and stormed out of the building. She barely even noticed as Hannibal and Oree, matching expressions of alarm on their faces, stepped out of her way to let her pass.

10

Wendi was not certain of much. Certainty was a luxury that some people could afford but not her. She had beliefs, she had ideas, but most of all, she had questions.

One thing that she was fairly sure of, not sure enough to be certain but sure enough to believe, was that she was originally from somewhere in the Inland Empire. There was really no reason for her belief but, more importantly, there was no reason not to believe it. In fact, she couldn't think of a single reason why she would feel so at home in the Inland Empire if she hadn't originally been from there. After all of the exploration she had done around the Inland Empire, and in some of the areas of the surrounding empires, she had come to that simple conclusion.

After all, the only place that could feel like home was home, wasn't it?

For most of the last five years, at every new town she arrived in, she had been searching for reports about missing people. She had collected thousands of reward posters and even more rumors during her search. One day, she was sure, she would find the missing piece of information that would tell her who she had been before she was Wendi.

Perhaps, she hoped, she would even discover where she was from.

"Was I married in my previous life?" she asked herself as she flipped through a stack of notes that she had already read through hundreds of times. "Did I have children?" She knew that her answers weren't in the stack of papers but as long as she was doing something, even something futile, she could convince herself that she was making progress.

She didn't even know if she was an alchemist back then.

She didn't even know what her name had been.

She had no idea what she had even looked like.

Without even the most basic of starting information, it had proven exceptionally difficult to find any information about her own personal history. As far as she could tell, she didn't have a life before the one she now led, which simply couldn't be possible, of that she was certain. Frustrated, she locked the papers back into her cabinet and headed for the stairs. "Too many questions," she said dejectedly. "And no answers"

There was only one way to get answers, and that was to go out and hunt for them. Just because the answers she sought hadn't appeared yet, that didn't mean that they weren't out there, waiting for her to uncover them.

She had spent much of her life, at least the life that she remembered, trying to not be jealous of the people who knew their own histories, people who could trace their lineage back generation upon generation, people who had friends they had known since childhood. Although she wouldn't give up Phemie, Crucian, and Jaegar for the world, she would give up just about anything else to discover even the simplest piece of information about herself. Only by knowing that, she believed, would she be able to start tracing what had befallen her.

As she walked across the courtyard toward the gate, she discovered that Sean hadn't left, despite her insistence that he do so. Instead, he was next to the barn, soothing a horse that had wandered a little too close to the caged gargoyles. One hand on the horse's neck and the other on its reins, he looked it squarely in one big eye and spoke quietly to it. Slowly, the horse calmed and he began to stroke its neck and mane, careful to keep a hand on it at all times.

As soon as the horse was calm enough to move, he led it into the barn. Both of them were out of sight so quickly Wendi blinked a couple times, wondering if she had just imagined it. The very idea of rough, abrasive Sean being able to soothe a panicking horse was almost too much for her to fathom. It simply didn't make any sense.

Why hadn't he gone home? she wondered. She had given him ample reason, even attacked him in front of tons of witnesses, a fact she was hardly proud of. Certainly his family hadn't forced him to return yet again after being treated so poorly, deserved as it may have been. If his intentions were to further annoy her, he was about to be sorely disappointed. She wasn't interested in staying home just to give him more opportunities to irritate her.

"Might as well start at the top," she decided as she reached the gate, focusing back onto the task at hand. The northernmost transport gate in the network was located in Vanguard, so she started her search there.

This was easily the furthest north Wendi had ever been and she was immediately thankful that she had worn her thick cloak. Despite the lateness of the season, it still felt very much as though it was still the dead of winter. Vanguard was filled with enormous, muscular barbarians who wore skins instead of the more traditional clothes with which she was more familiar and made some of the best wine Wendi had ever tasted. They also had a thick, heady stout that was even more pungent than Greystone mead, which was a feat unto itself. The people of Vanguard were rambunctious and friendly, and though the weather was cool, she warmed up to them immediately.

They lived in long-houses, each of which was almost three times as long as a standard home from the Inland Sea but were only a single room wide. Their taverns, which they called mead halls, were shaped roughly the same way. A single table ran down the length of the hall and people sat and stood as they saw fit. Bawdy tunes were sung completely out of tune and overlapping one another. Laughter erupted from everywhere and more than once Wendi saw exuberant revelers climb up onto the table and dance for a few steps before falling off again.

Twice, eager young men picked her up as though to carry her off for the night but when she told them she wasn't interested, they put her back down and found someone else to carry off.

In the morning, she considered heading down to talk to the town's leader but decided against it. As much fun as the previous night's frivolity had been, she had known as soon as she arrived that she was not a Vanguardian. Instead, she headed for the next town on her list.

Hodgman was a small town on the northern bank of the Pirate Run. It was desolate and run-down and she wondered how people could live in a hovel like that. Half of the buildings in town looked like the only thing holding them from complete collapse was wishful thinking and the rest looked like they had already been knocked over, only to have another shanty dropped on top of it.

"Spare a coin, miss?" an urchin called out from the side of the street. Wendi couldn't tell whether the child was male or female but it appeared to be no older than ten. Feeling sorry for the situation the poor child was in, she handed over a thaler. She knew a copper coin wouldn't get very far, even in a town as poverty-stricken as this one but she hoped it would provide at least one warm meal.

Placement of a transport gate to encourage business didn't seem to have helped much. If it had helped, she wasn't sure she wanted to know how bad the town's economy had been before the gate's arrival. Without looking too deeply into the town's shops, she headed for the town magistrate to make her inquiries.

"Missing person?" He asked as he began to chuckle. "Lady, this here town's on the Pirate Run. We've got missing people the way other towns have grass in their fields!"

Despite his comments, he handed over a stack of papers, each of which contained information about a person who had been reported missing. Wendi shuffled through the stack, immediately eliminating men and children. Although she still had no idea who she was, she was absolutely positive that she was fully grown and female. She handed the eliminated suspects back to the magistrate and tucked the remainder into her pocket for later perusal.

From there, feeling more desolate than she had when she first started, she went to a small town called Dent, about a day's travel north of the Inland Sea. She had been there on a similar quest years before, so she had little hope that she would find the answers she sought there.

She wasn't disappointed. The officials in Dent didn't have anything more to add than what she had already gotten. With nothing more to find there, she continued to the next location in the network.

Hub, the center of all trade in the Inland Empire, finally had a transport gate installed as well. Eagerly, she changed course and headed there. If anywhere would have answers for her, Hub would be it.

Hub was a large, stepped island in the middle of the Inland Sea. Because of that, it was the first stop every ship made when leaving the Sea and the last stop before heading back to whichever port they hailed from. Even better, it had a portal, which connected it to far more places than Wendi could hope to reach on her own by just using the transport gate network. She scampered from the magistrate's office to the courthouse to the local loremaster in search of answers but again turned up nothing of value. For two days, she spoke to everyone who would speak to her but while she gathered a thick stack of papers and notes on far more missing people than she was comfortable hearing about, she was not optimistic about any of it. Despite the sheer quantity of her findings, none of them seemed like they could have been her.

As she headed back for the gate to head home, she glanced at the docks and discovered that the ship Temptress was in town. Temptress was the flagship of McClannahan trading and its captain was rumored to be the owner of the company. Wendi had never heard back from the message she had left for him in Hoem but the opportunity was just too good to miss.

John McClannahan was a gruff, dour, middle-aged seaman but Wendi knew better than to judge a person by how they looked. She walked boldly up to him and offered a hand. "My name is Wendi," she introduced herself. "I own Dragon Keep."

Obviously surprised by her direct greeting, he took her hand and shook it. "Heard of you," he nodded. "Heard my nephew's been working for you." She tried to keep the reactionary expression from her face, but he saw it nonetheless. His eyes twinkled as he began to chuckle. "Yeah, I guess 'working' is a bit too strong of a word for it, hmm?"

"I wasn't coming here to talk with you about Sean," she explained. "I was hoping to talk business."

He looked at her for a long moment before nodding. "Let me finish up with the dockmaster and I'll be right with you." He turned and yelled at a tall, fair-haired man. "Dane! Buy the lady a drink and keep her company until I'm done."

The attractive blonde's eyes lit up at the order and he hurried over to where Wendi was waiting. "There's a tavern just up this way," he smiled at her genteelly and offered her an arm. "I'll be happy to escort you there."

She accepted his arm, not because she wanted to but to be polite. John had obviously wanted her to accompany him but she was already turned off by the young man, attractive though he may be. He walked with the easy swagger of a man who expected to be admired and she had to admit that it worked. Admiring glances followed him as he walked and she actually heard one young girl sigh when he smiled at her.

Seriously, she thought to herself, *who does that?*

"So," Dane said as he held the door for her at the tavern and led her to a table. "You're John's lady friend, then." He made it sound like a statement rather than a question and she was taken aback by it.

"Actually," she said carefully as she accepted the glass of rich burgundy wine, "I'm here to talk business with him."

Dane's smile deepened as he looked at her, and Wendi was thankful that her cloak covered well more than it really should have. The man simply oozed with pheromones. What she would give, she mused, to bottle some of it. Added to one of Phemie's philters, they would be unstoppable. "What kind of business?"

"I run a merchant shop south of Three Rivers," she explained. "I was hoping that we could come to a mutually beneficial arrangement." She took another sip of her wine, wishing John would hurry. Dane was far too friendly for her taste. Too friendly and too pretty. She had never been fond of pretty men.

To her relief, although John seemed to be taking an inordinately long time, a familiar person walked into the tavern before she was halfway through with her drink. Oree's grandfather, Cookie, spotted her and Dane and smiled broadly, heading immediately over to their table. "Wendi," Cookie greeted her. "So nice to see you again. How have you been?" Without waiting for an invitation, he pulled out a chair and took a seat. "What brings you to town?"

"I was here doing some research," she explained. "But when I saw the Temptress was here, I had to see if I could have a word with the captain."

Dane looked back and forth between Wendi and Cookie in surprise. "You two know each other?" he asked finally.

"Sure we do," Cookie included Dane in his smile. "This is Wendi, from Dragon Keep. She's the one who bought the boys from slavery."

Dane's expression of surprise only deepened. "You're the dragon lady?"

"That was rude," Cookie cut in sharply.

"No," Wendi smiled. "It's all right." She had heard the rumor that her keep was called Dragon Keep because she was really a dragon posing as a human. Rather than being offended, she was amused by the stories. Offensive as the rumors may sound, they were far better than some of the other things she had been called.

"So how are the boys?" Cookie turned his attention back to her. "Are they behaving?"

"Oree is wonderful," she admitted, surprised to find that it was true. Even after seeing what she looked like beneath the hood, Oree had never given any indication of the repulsion most people experienced. "And so is Hannibal. They finally finished cleaning out the inn, so that's about to open."

Cookie's smile faded. "What about Sean? I heard there was a bit of trouble with you a while back."

"Sean is..." she searched to find the right words to describe how annoying, how obnoxious, how thoroughly infuriating he was but couldn't. "He's Sean."

Conversation turned to more mundane topics until John finally came wandering in to the tavern. After stopping at the bar for a drink of his own, he came over to take a seat at their table. Dane left almost immediately, a fact that didn't surprise Wendi in the slightest. "So. What can I do for you?" John asked as he settled comfortably in his seat.

"As I mentioned earlier," she explained, "I own Dragon Keep, where there is a small trading shop. We specialize in unusual, exotic goods and items that can be used for magical spellcasting and other componentry. As you are one of the largest and furthest-reaching traders in the Inland Empire, I would like the opportunity to open trading with you."

He took another drink and eyed her thoughtfully. "Does that mean you're wanting to buy goods from me or sell goods to me?"

"A little bit of both, actually." She smiled and continued. "I'm sure you see a lot more unusual items than what would normally pass through my keep, items that may be common in other areas but far less so in the Inland Empire. I would like the chance to look through your inventory on occasion to see if there is anything that fits my needs."

"That sounds reasonable enough," he agreed. "What kinds of things would you want to sell in return?"

"I have a handful of items that are unique to Dragon Keep." She explained about her two flavors of alchemically-augmented chewing gum, which had turned out to be far more popular than she had expected. She also explained about the snakewine and a handful of other spirits and alchemical and magical concoctions that she and her crew had developed.

He listened attentively, tapping a finger against his glass as she spoke. "Of course, I'd have to be able to verify your claims on these things," he said once she was finished. "I can't just go around telling my customers about something that I haven't personally experienced."

"Of course," she agreed. "I could bring an assortment to you the next time you are in Hoem," she offered. "But it may be easier for you to come to the Keep and peruse what we have for yourself. You may find something interesting that I hadn't expected you to want to see."

He agreed that her idea sounded reasonable and promised to come up to Dragon Keep to check her stock as soon as he returned to Hoem. Satisfied that she had made a very valuable contact, she thanked him for both his time and the drink.

Empty-handed but feeling much more content than she had before leaving on her trip, she headed back home. Although there were still a lot of places left on her list of places to inquire about missing persons, those locations could wait until her next trip.

At the keep, she discovered that business had slowly but steadily increased in her absence. A handful of adventuring parties had stopped in to sell some of their findings and Phemie had placed another chalkboard in the shop, requesting creatures – dead or alive – from any adventurers who wanted to make some extra sheckles.

"What's this for?" Wendi asked when she spotted the sign. "Dead makes sense, depending on the animal, but we don't have anywhere to store living creatures."

"Remy helped with that," Phemie explained, naming one of the people responsible for the transport gate network with whom she and Wendi had a friendship. "He really liked the idea of us having a menagerie, particularly because there is actually a branch of studies at the academy on magical creatures, so that will draw in more students, too."

Wendi hadn't known about that branch of studies, so her optimism about the increased draw to Dragon Keep by the menagerie increased at the news. *Maybe*, she thought, *other magical students and teachers from other academies will eventually come to see our collection*. It was a nice thought, although not one she was about to put any stock into any time soon. But it never hurt to have plans for the future.

Even Sean, Oree, and Hannibal had been doing their part to pitch in around the keep, to one degree or another. While Wendi had been gone, they had made progress in cleaning out another of the abandoned buildings. She had no idea what she would do with it once it was clear but the less work that Crucian and Jaegar had to do, the better.

Of course, Hannibal and Oree had been doing the lion's share of the work. As usual, Sean had found a comfortable place next to the stables to sit back and watch the bustling merchants. He was perched on one of the hitching posts, heels of his boots tucked beneath him against the brass ring for balance while he rested. Wendi wasn't sure whether he hadn't noticed her arrival or if he chose to act as though he hadn't.

She was really wishing that she had just left him in the stocks.

11

That night, after Wendi dropped off the purchases she had made on her journey, she picked up a meal and took it upstairs to her suite. She didn't feel like being around a lot of people and needed a little bit of quiet time to digest what she had learned in her wandering – or rather, what she hadn't learned. She had a collection of notices about missing people and a few hints and rumors that she had managed to gather but most of it was of no real value to her. Not that she had expected much more than what she had found, of course. The ever-widening gap of time between when she had disappeared from her previous life and when she made each round of inquiries only lessened the chance of her finding something viable.

Memories fade, she understood. Even people who weren't missing enormous chunks of their past experienced the dimness of time. Soon, she knew, there would no longer be a point to her continued search.

Everything she had once been would have been forgotten.

A knock on her door startled her as she set her plate down on her small table. She glanced at her cloak, debating whether she should put it on, but then realized there was no reason to. It was probably Phemie with another question or Crucian wanting another bottle of snakewine. Perhaps she should just stick an entire snake in a bottle of wine and give that to him, it may help to mitigate his demands for more wine. Unless, of course, he decided he liked it.

To her surprise, it was neither. Hannibal stood on the other side of her door, his massive form almost filing the hallway. She blinked at him in surprise. "What are you doing here?"

"I was hoping to talk to you," he explained. "I didn't get a chance to say anything before you left."

She stepped aside and motioned for him to enter. Closing the door behind him, she asked, "What's on your mind?"

"I just wanted to apologize for the way Sean's been acting," he said. "I know he can be a jerk sometimes but some of the things he said to you were out of line."

"There's no reason for you to apologize," she stopped him before he went any further. "You haven't done anything to be apologizing for and Sean's a grown man. You don't need to be sorry on his behalf.

"Not that it matters, really. You guys will all be going home in a few days anyway."

He looked over at her, startled by her announcement. "I thought we owed you a lot, still."

"You and Oree have been doing a lot more than I had expected around here," she shrugged. "And as far as Sean goes, I'm willing to forgive the debt and take the loss just to be rid of him. So you can all look forward to going back to your lives soon."

He stood in surprised silence for a long moment before nodding. "Thank you," he said finally. "For buying us out of debt and for letting us work it off the way you have." He turned as though ready to leave.

"I do like what you've done with this keep," he pointed out as he reached the door. "I remember years ago when it was just a crumbling old ruin that nobody wanted to go near. It's nice to see that someone cares about the old place." He glanced back at her again. "You must have some pretty strong motivations for fixing this old place up instead of just finding somewhere that isn't just a wreck."

She laughed at his comment. "When you can't call anywhere else home," she said, "it's easier to just make a home of your own. If that home happens to be in the middle of nowhere in a crumbling old ruin, then so be it." She met his warm brown eyes with her own cold black ones, as if to underscore her point. She wasn't accepted in any towns, she knew. She never would be.

Hannibal looked as though he was about to ask more questions of her, so she deftly reached around him to open the door. She held it as he stepped into the hallway. "Go let your friends know they can look forward to going home soon."

He still looked like he had more on his mind as she closed the door. What she had told Cookie had been true; she liked Hannibal. However, he was feeling far too comfortable around her, which his arrival at her door could attest. When people became comfortable, they began to ask questions, and there were some questions that she just couldn't answer.

With a sigh, she sat down to her meal. At least Jaegar hadn't prepared it, she realized.

It was cooked.

Per Wendi's request, Phemie hired a few new people. They needed someone to run the newly-established inn, which Wendi still hadn't settled on a name for, and more people to help in the shop and tavern. More people coming to shop at Dragon Keep was great for business but it had been getting harder to keep up with the increased traffic.

"We need more snakewine," Krun, one of the new tavern-keepers, explained to Wendi when she stopped in for her morning meal. "Someone started a rumor that drinking the venomous wines would help increase a man's virility." Wendi didn't have to wonder where that rumor had come from. Phemie had a definite set of ideas about what would cause a man to buy strange things and virility was one of her favorite selling points.

"Anything else we're running low on?"

"Not that I know of. I can do an inventory check and let you know."

Phemie had been able to keep up with the demand for her potions and philters but some of the alchemical creations were at alarmingly low levels. To rebuild her supply, Wendi sequestered herself in her lab and got all of her equipment running at as close to full capacity as she could. First of all, however, she needed to distill some more venom.

As she unlocked her toxin cabinet, she looked at the assortment thoughtfully. She had far more venoms than just the one she used for

snakewine and if men were buying it to increase their virility, as unlikely as it seemed, then perhaps she could expand her line of venom-
enhanced drinks. She pulled out vials of spider and scorpion venoms as
well, curious as to what effect those would have.

Wendi's views on business were simple. She didn't discriminate
with her clientele, so as long as a person had tyros to spend, they were
welcome. She was willing to do business with anyone and everyone, so
long as they behaved and didn't irritate any of her staff enough to be
thrown out. For the most part, the purchases her customers made were
innocuous, picking and choosing from the selection on her shelves. A
small handful of people knew that there were more shelves, stocked
with far more dangerous items, hidden behind a sturdy wooden door
at the back of the shop.

That back room was where the toxins and antitoxins, the more
powerful versions of some of Phemie's potions, and the components
that were not openly discussed were stored. For the customers who
needed the hair of a murderer, the blood of a mermaid, or the skin
of a firehound, there was only one readily available place where they
could be purchased and that was in the back room of her shop. None of
the things she carried were against the law, technically, but they were
all items that, had everyone known about them, would have lost her
almost as much business as the taboo items brought in.

Tolerant as she was of people who worked best under cover of night,
she accepted absolutely no nonsense in her keep. Anyone caught acting
dangerously was asked to leave, immediately and without exception.
For those who were unwilling to leave voluntarily, Crucian provided
adequate encouragement for them to vacate. If they still refused, he
was more than capable of throwing them bodily out of the Keep. After
all, giant squid ink ceases to be useful once it has been spilled onto the
floor and a Hand of Glory held no value whatsoever once it has been
set on fire.

Besides just the people hired to help with the businesses, Phemie
had also hired a handful of thieves to watch out for disappearing
merchandise. Somehow, and Wendi didn't have the slightest clue how

she had done it, she had convinced a small group of cutpurses and fast-hands that they wanted to help catch and guard against thievery. One of the nearby guilds had apparently decided that Dragon Keep would prove an easy target and Phemie was determined to convince them otherwise.

The gargoyles in cages behind the shop had already proven to be a much bigger attraction than she had anticipated. As word spread that a live gargoyle was available to view, people flocked to Dragon Keep just to see them, sometimes staying a night at the inn but usually stopping in the tavern for a meal and drinks. Having a live gargoyle in the back courtyard was absolutely worth it, in Wendi's opinion, so long as it kept bringing more people to the keep.

Although she had initially agreed to the idea of starting a menagerie, Wendi had been holding on to some doubts. Given the draw from the gargoyles, however, she was beginning to come more and more around to the thought that maybe the idea of starting a menagerie wasn't such a bad one after all. While the toxins distilled, she unrolled a map and tacked it to her wall. There were a lot of creatures scattered throughout the Inland Empire, many of which she already kept track of for her own resupply runs, and she began marking places on the map where she knew they could be found. There were more goatsuckers outside of Landor, she was sure, and capturing a Stillok spider wouldn't be that hard, as long as she took plenty of antitoxin with her.

The more she thought about it, the more merit the idea gained. By having some of these creatures at the Keep, she would be able to milk their venom or shear their hair occasionally, lessening the need for hunting. She could gather a lot of what she needed in her own backyard. It wasn't exactly like she was lacking in room to store them, either, as the keep was far larger than she had any reasonable expectation of ever using otherwise.

"Maybe getting them in pairs would be better," she thought, but quickly dismissed the idea. The last thing she wanted was for things to start breeding. Except, of course, in cases where the young of a creature were particularly valuable. Gryphon eggs and gryphon young were some of the most valuable items that she hadn't yet been able to get in stock, for good reason.

There were some creatures she wouldn't be able to add to the collection, of course. A roc was simply too big to cage successfully; they were nearly as large as the Keep. Other creatures were too big as well and still more were too small. However, there were plenty that were large enough without being too large and exotic enough but not so rare that she wouldn't be able to find one. Those, she was sure, she could gather and bring home.

12

"Hold its mouth closed!" Wendi yelled to Jaegar as the enormous red and brown lizard thrashed wildly. "The last thing we need is this cursed thing burning down half the keep." The lizard was almost thirty feet long from the tip of its snout to the end of its tail, cramped inside the fifteen-foot-long transport cage.

"I got it," Jaegar said through gritted teeth as he threw one arm over and the other under the creature's snapping jaws. Locking one hand around the opposite wrist, he strained and his biceps bulged beneath his tunic sleeves as the creature fought to bite him.

The lizard was a fire-breathing Ignus lizard that Wendi had found south of Kowleun. It hadn't been happy when she and Crucian trapped it in the wagon's cage and was even less happy that it was now being pulled back out of it. The musky smell emanating from it was telltale, as it evidenced the creature's distress. Luckily there weren't any free-roaming Ignus lizards nearby, as Wendi had discovered the hard way that the scent attracted more lizards, each of them ready and willing to attack.

"I've got the door open," Crucian added helpfully. His tunic was bunched up at his chest, where his left arm was tied to his chest in a sling. The Ignus lizard had broken his forearm and bitten off a chunk of flesh the first time they had tried to pull it out of its cage, which was why Phemie had a thick leather strap at the ready. As soon as Jaegar had a good enough grip on the creature's maw, the diminutive witch darted inside the cage, wrapped the leather strap around the lizard's mouth just ahead of Jaegar's straining arms and cinched it tight. Just to be safe, she pulled a second strap out of her belt and tightened it around the creature just behind where Jaegar still held it.

"Okay," Wendi said as soon as both straps were secure, "let's pull it out." While Jaegar had been fighting to keep his grip on the lizard and Phemie was strapping it, Wendi had been holding onto the creature's hindquarters. Its tail was twice as long as its body and was thrashing about furiously. It had already knocked Wendi asunder a couple times but it hadn't done enough damage to keep her down. Now, all they had to do was drag the irate Ignus backwards from the transport cage and into the waiting fireproof box that would be its new home.

The lizard dug its claws into the bottom of the cage, locking into place and refusing to budge. Wendi wished that Crucian's arm had been undamaged; she could have really used his strength right then. But there was nothing she could do about his arm, which would ail him for about a week before being good as new, she knew. She didn't have a week to wait for him, though, the cage holding the Ignus wasn't strong enough to hold it for that long.

"Need a hand?" Strong arms reached past her and grabbed the creature's back pair of legs, pulling them out from beneath it and setting the lizard thrashing around again. Taking those claws out of play made a big difference and between Wendi, Jaegar, Phemie, and whoever had joined them to help, they managed to drag the Ignus lizard back out of the cage and drop it into its new home.

Wendi didn't bother sending anyone into the cage to retrieve the straps. The Ignus was storming around its new home, snarling and clawing at its face in an attempt to remove the binding leather. It would be free soon enough and the small cost of the straps was cheap compared to the damage it would do to whoever went in after them.

"Thanks for the help," she said as she wiped her hands off on her cloak and readjusted the hood. It had moved quite a bit during the struggle and she needed to put it back into place before anyone saw her. "We really appreciate..." Her voice trailed off as she discovered who had been assisting her.

Sean grinned at her, cocky as ever. "No problem," he said. "You know me, always glad to help."

Her appreciative smile faded. It had been more than three months since she had sent the men home and she hadn't been surprised in the slightest when none of them came back to visit. Cookie had stopped in once, arriving with John when he came up to peruse her shop but Sean, Oree, and Hannibal had made themselves scarce.

"What are you doing here?" Wendi asked coldly, all traces of delight gone from her voice. "I didn't think I'd see any of you again." She scanned the visible areas of the keep as she spoke but she didn't see Oree or Hannibal anywhere. "And where are your sidekicks?"

His grin faded as well and he looked at her sheepishly. It wasn't an expression she had ever seen on him before and it didn't suit him at all. It unsettled her, like seeing a gargoyle break into a fit of giggles.

It just wasn't supposed to happen.

"They aren't here," he answered. "It's just me."

"Well, if it's snakewine you're after, you know where the tavern is." She tried to step past him, but he reached out and took her by the arm.

"I need to talk to you." His voice was serious, as was his expression. The sheepishness was gone, but so was the cockiness. If anything, he looked worried.

"What about?"

"I was hoping that I could finish paying off the debt I owe you." When she started to protest, he nodded. "I know, you said all of our debts were forgiven. We all appreciate that but I need to come back and actually finish paying mine."

She looked at him, dumbfounded. "Why would I want to do that?" she asked. "What makes you think I'd ever want to put up with you again, now that I've finally gotten rid of you?"

"I know I was awful," he said, his eyes earnest. "And you didn't deserve that. But I want to make it right with you."

Something was terribly wrong, she knew. People didn't just change their minds, their whole attitudes, that quickly. "Why?" she asked, suspicion dripping freely from her voice. "Making things right didn't matter three months ago, why should it matter now?"

"Because it's the only option I've got," he answered. Far from his usual arrogance, his voice verged on desperate. She wondered what could have happened to him. "Can we talk about this somewhere else, please?"

As he spoke, she became aware of the people who surrounded them. Phemie, Crucian and Jaegar were there, of course, pulling the last of Wendi's goods from the wagon. Others had come to see the latest addition to the menagerie as well so they were almost completely surrounded by curious onlookers.

"Fine," she relented, against her better judgement, and handed him a leather pouch. "I need to take these to my lab anyway. Come with me." The pouch contained fire sacs, the glands that allowed the Ignus lizards to breathe fire. The glands produced a noxious chemical that ignited when it contacted air so she had put the sacs into the leather pouch to keep them airtight during transport. The sacs in the pouch had come from the three lizards that she hadn't been able to capture alive. Their carcasses were still on the back of the wagon, waiting to be unloaded.

Sean followed her down the steep stone stairs that led to her lab. He looked around in amazement at all of her equipment and sketches. "What is all this stuff?" he asked.

"Why is it so important that you come back here?" she asked, taking the pouch from him and setting it carefully onto one of her shelves while ignoring his question. "You said you wanted private; this is about as private as it gets here. So tell me or get out."

"My mother wants me to get married," he explained. "She already has a girl picked out and everything. When I came home last time, she said I'd had enough time running around the countryside and it was time to settle down."

"What does that have to do with me?" she asked. "Seems like your mother's got the right idea." She smiled humorlessly. "Besides, if you're home with your wife, you won't end up in a slaver's pen again."

"But I don't want to get married," he said, his voice more forceful than before, "especially this way. If I do get married, I want it to be because I actually care about the woman, not because she wants to be a McClannahan." He spat the last word out with such vehemence that Wendi was taken aback.

"So talk to your father," she said gently. "I'm sure he would understand your position."

"I tried that." He raked his hand through his orange-red hair. "But he said that I have to uphold the family image and that its time I started to act the way I was supposed to." He looked at her pleadingly. "He said my only options were to marry Hethere or to come back here until my debt was paid in full."

She could understand his predicament. Not only was Sean a McClannahan, one of the most influential families in the Inland Empire, he was the son of the mayor. And, as far as she knew, the eldest of all the McClannahan boys. Women had been known to vie for years to land a husband such as him, ill-tempered or not. On one hand, she really didn't want to bring him back to Dragon Keep, not doubting for a moment that he would revert to his usual lazy ways but he looked so pitiful that she couldn't in good conscience say no.

"If you're going to be here," she responded after thinking her options over for a few moments, "you're going to work. Not sit in the tavern and drink, not sit in the sun and watch others do the work for you. Is that understood?"

The smile that broke over his face in relief lit him up like a sunrise after a long storm. "Thank you," he said. "Anything you need, I'm right here."

"For starters," she answered, "you can go muck out the stable." It was the dirtiest, smelliest job in the entire keep and she knew that she had sent him to clean it out of sheer spite but she didn't care. Nor did she feel bad about it. For all the trouble he had already caused her, a little bit of stink was more than warranted.

To her amazement, he went and mucked out the stall. Furthermore, he did it without argument, and made no argument for the series of chores she assigned to him once he was done. Perhaps he was able to work after all, she mused to herself a few days later as she hauled yet another box from her lab to the tavern.

"...so all you have to do is blow nice and gently until the bubble bursts and you'll have a spectacular bolt of lightning to scare your friends with."

Phemie was explaining to yet another customer how to use the chewing gum while Wendi walked past her with a case of her new scorpion-venom wine. Unlike the snakewine, which was a pale yellow color, the scorpion blend was a deep, violent burgundy. The case she carried was the only case she had left after Crucian found her stash and drank himself into a venom-infused stupor. He was still in his room of the main building, sleeping off the aftereffects, and that had been from the drinking binge two days ago.

Wendi had diluted the venom further after that. If it was strong enough to knock the part-troll off his feet, it was probably too potent for regular humans.

"Where is my fiancée?" A petite, pale-haired girl wearing a summer-weight dress under an embroidered cloak demanded as she stormed into the shop. "I know he's here somewhere. Where is he?"

"Well, that would depend," Wendi answered casually. "Who is your fiancée?"

"As if you don't know," the young woman snapped at her. "I'm looking for Sean and you have him hidden somewhere."

"Oh," Wendi answered, unimpressed with the girl's lack of manners. "He's working." The girl must be Hethere, she decided.

She only got a single step further before Hethere moved to intercept her again. "I don't care what he's doing," she explained. "I want to see him now. Bring him to me."

"No." Wendi was beginning to understand why Sean didn't want to marry the girl. Two days ago, she wouldn't have suspected it was possible but she was even worse than he was. "As I said, he's working. If you want to wait, you can see him after he's done for the day. But until then, you'll just have to wait."

"Now you listen to me," Hethere said, her voice much louder, as Wendi moved to walk past her again. "I happen to be the mayor of Hoem's soon-to-be daughter. If you want to continue doing business with anyone in the McClannahan family, you'd better bring Sean me to at once!" Her volume had increased with every word so that at the end, she was practically screaming.

The shop fell silent at the girl's outburst and Wendi had to resist the urge to snap back at the irritating visitor. There was no reason that she should have to put up with this kind of nonsense, particularly within her own keep. Rather than striking out at her, however, she took a slow, calming breath.

"I don't particularly care who you are or what you want," she explained calmly, much more calmly than she felt. "But threatening me will do you absolutely no good whatsoever. As I said, if you want to wait until Sean's done working for the day, you can see him then. Otherwise, you can take yourself back to Hoem and whine to your friends.

"I, on the other hand, have better things to do than sit here and watch you act like a fool." Without another word and without giving Hethere a chance to respond, she stepped around the open-mouthed girl and headed for the tavern.

"Krun," she called out as she stepped into the building, "I've got a new batch of wine for you."

Sean found her in her lab a couple hours later. "Are you busy?" he asked as he watched her add a measured amount of yellow-green fluid to one of her distillation vats.

"No more than usual," she answered. "What's on your mind?"

"Phemie told me that Hethere stopped in earlier and threw a fit. I wanted to thank you for intercepting her before she found me."

Wendi nodded, pulling more supplies from her shelves. "I can understand why your mother picked her for you." She picked a cask of benzoin gum up from the floor where she had tucked it under her worktable and set it aside. "She's just like you."

He looked, slack-jawed, at her. "I am nothing like that girl."

"You have been acting like a spoiled, entitled little prat since the day I met you." She met his eyes and added, "I didn't send her away to make your life easier. I sent her away because people like that irritate me."

13

"Do you carry any artifacts?" A young-looking man with dark brown hair and vibrant blue eyes caught Wendi's arm as she walked through the shop.

"A few," she responded automatically. "What kind of artifact are you looking for?" She carefully removed her arm from his hand, not wanting to offend the inquiring customer.

"It's an old family heirloom," he explained, tucking his thumbs into his belt and smiling at her. His smile was charming, even if there was something about the man that disturbed her. Everything about him screamed a combination of powerful, possibly magically-augmented charisma and danger. Most commonly attributed to charlatans, it was not a combination that Wendi found appealing. "It's a drinking horn," he continued. "Made from the horn of a unicorn. It's set into a pewter base that has four large garnets set into it."

Wendi shook her head slowly. "I haven't seen anything like that come through here."

"Please," he reached for her arm once more, but she moved out of the way before he could touch her. From the corner of her eye, she spotted Crucian moving closer to intercept the eager young man and escort him out if necessary but Wendi waved a hand for him to be patient. Just because she didn't like the man, that didn't immediately mean that she couldn't do business with him.

"It was stolen from my family a number of years ago," he explained, tucking his thumbs back into his belt. "So when I heard that you guys carry a lot of unusual and unique items, I wanted to come see for myself." He grinned at her again. "I had hoped that whoever had stolen it from us may have sold it to you."

"I haven't seen it," Wendi repeated herself, "but I'll keep an eye out for it." Even as she responded, she ran a mental checklist of everything in the illicit goods section of the store, already knowing that they had nothing like what he was describing in stock. Wendi had never even heard of such an item.

"Wonderful!" The man beamed at her. He explained which inn he was staying at in Three Rivers and requested her to send word to him if she heard anything about his family heirloom. Wendi agreed to do so, with absolutely no intentions of following through on such. The man was either a confidence man or a charlatan of some other variety and she had no inclination to get caught up in whatever scheme he was trying to pull. His story of being in search of a family heirloom sounded just a little too easy and Wendi had spent just a little too much time around thieves lately to fall for his words so easily.

"While I'm here," he said as he turned to leave, "I don't suppose you have any unicorn horns by themselves, do you?" he looked back at her and smiled. "My mother was devastated at the loss, so if I can't find the horn, I'd like to be able to remanufacture it if I could. That way, she can be at peace while I continue to search."

"Unicorns are extinct," Wendi explained patiently. "We haven't had any come through our shop but if any do show up, we'll be sure to let you know."

The man cast another glance around the shop before nodding to himself and leaving. Wendi turned to go back to her lab, where she had been heading before she had been intercepted but she was stopped yet again as Sean stepped next to her.

"What is it?" she asked in exasperation. "I've got work to do." She briefly wondered if this was another ploy on his part to get out of doing his work but quickly shook it off. Since his return, almost none of his previous bad habits had resurfaced.

"I know," he said as he walked alongside her toward her lab. "But I'm concerned over the guy you were just talking to."

"What concern?" she asked. "He's gone." She wondered if Sean had gotten the same feeling of unease from the visitor as she had and, if so, what it meant.

"Yes, but I think I've heard of an artifact like the one he was asking about." She looked up at him in surprise, so he continued. "While Hannibal, Oree and I were out exploring, we heard rumors about an old drinking horn that sounded a lot like the one he was after."

"So the family heirloom sparked some rumors," she shrugged. "That's hardly new." She couldn't count the amount of time she had wasted following similar rumors about legendary artifacts that turned out to be nothing whatsoever outside of tall tales. Everyone wanted their precious things to have greater importance than they rightfully had.

"This one wasn't just any old family heirloom," he said quietly as he followed her down the stairs. "It was known as the Horn of Ascension and it belonged to the emperor of the Dracott Empire."

That got her attention. She stopped at the bottom of the steps and looked up at him in amazement. "A royal relic?" she asked breathlessly. If a regal item like that had turned up missing, she wanted to find it indeed. When ruling families lost their heirlooms, they generally offered a substantial reward for their return. Moreover, a lot of other people would be willing to pay even more handsomely to own them. Anything having to do with a royal family was automatically worth a lot of money to a collector.

"But why would someone be looking for it out here?" she asked finally. "The Dracott Empire is all the way on the other side of the Azul Sea."

Sean headed back up the stairs after offering to see what other information he could gather on the horn. Once he was gone, however, Wendi continued to think about the unusual artifact. Even if the rumor Sean had told her about turned out to be false, she didn't care. Unicorns had been hunted to extinction long before her time so the chances of her getting her hands on a real unicorn's horn, no matter what condition it was in, appealed to her greatly. There were hundreds, perhaps even thousands of people who would pay tons of tyros to get their hands on one.

Even a broken shard from an authentic unicorn horn was worth its weight in gold.

Almost as exciting as the unicorn horn itself was the description of the pewter and garnet base that the blue-eyed man had explained the horn sat in. Pewter wasn't all that special, there were plenty of skilled pewter smiths around. However, garnets were only found in one region, which happened to be in the Dracott Empire and they were carefully guarded by those who had them. All that meant was that while the garnets on the base weren't quite as rare as the horn itself, they came a close second.

It also meant that if the relic he had inquired about was genuine, the odds were high that it actually was a regal item from the Dracott Empire as Sean had suggested. She leaned against the wall just outside her lab, picturing what it would be like to hold an authentic regal relic such as that in her own hands. It was such a fantastic thought that she could barely picture it.

If she did, by some miracle, come across the horn, she wouldn't go out of her way to inform the man who had alerted her to its existence in the first place. Something about him, she couldn't quite place her mind on what particularly it had been, had rankled her. She almost never took an immediate dislike to anyone but she had taken one to him.

14

The following day, Sean returned to Hoem to take a day off and visit with his friends and family. He had been at Dragon Keep for almost a month but though Oree and Hannibal had both come to see him, he had been unable to spend much time with them. Hethere had come as well but to Wendi's relief, she had been much better behaved on every visit after the first one.

Of course, behaving better than she had been was not the same as being well behaved.

"Do you want me to check with John if he's in town to see if he's heard any rumors?" Sean offered as he was getting ready to leave. "He travels all over the place, so he might have heard something I hadn't."

"No," she answered, "it's fine. You're supposed to be resting. Say hello to the guys for me, if you would."

"All right," he agreed. For a moment, it looked as though he was going to say something else, but then he changed his mind. "I'll see you in a couple days, then."

"No, you won't," she said without looking up from her notes. "I have to leave for a little while and I doubt I'll return inside a week."

"Where are you going?" His brows were lowered in concern. "If you're getting more creatures for the menagerie, I can come with you."

"It's nothing like that," she reassured him, finally looking up to meet his eyes. Since she was in her lab, she wasn't wearing her cloak. Instead, it hung on the small tin hook just behind her door. He didn't flinch when his eyes met hers as he had done the first time. Even after seeing her obsidian stare, he had been unnerved by it for a little while but had made a concentrated effort not to show how much it disturbed him. Over the last while, however, either he had gotten much better at not showing his reaction or it had simply ceased to bother him. She wasn't sure which of the possibilities was true but whichever it was, she was glad for it.

She should be used to the reactions from people, she knew, but it still bothered her a lot more than she wanted to admit. "I'm going up to Burgard for more whale oil for the lamps." Though not completely true, it wasn't a lie, either. Jaegar had made a point of telling her that they were running low again. However, the main reason she was eager to head to Burgard was because of its proximity to the Dracott Empire.

She had made some inquiries of her own and discovered that there was indeed supposedly a drinking horn made from the spire of a unicorn that was used to determine the rulers of the Dracott Empire. Whoever could produce the Horn of Ascension would automatically be crowned the next emperor. Burgard was as close as she could get to the source of the Horn of Ascension, so it was the obvious place to start.

If Sean's rumors and the others that she had uncovered were true, there were two places that she could look. However, only one of her two options had a transport gate.

Burgard, as with all of the northern towns, was very much like Vanguard. The buildings were narrow and long, the people were tall and broad. They subsided primarily from their whaling business, selling whale oil and other trappings to all of the surrounding areas. Quite a few more people than Wendi had expected to see roamed the streets and most of them weren't even northmen. People from all around the Inland Empire had come to the northern town to buy oil, furs, bones, and candles.

She spent a few days in town asking for information about the Horn of Ascension from almost everyone she came across but precious few had anything of value to tell her. Most of the northmen didn't concern themselves with the affairs of the other empires and even less so with the ruling families and their trinkets.

Without any better options, she headed for Tradewinds.

Tradewinds was a large island that sat far into the Azul Sea. It was just south of the Sea's entrance to the Pirate Run but about a day's travel further out into the Sea. Boats frequently stopped at the island for, much as how Hub was the center of trade for the Inland Sea, Tradewinds was one of the most common centers of business within the Azul Sea. While it had a portal, Wendi was dismayed to learn that it had not yet received a transport gate.

Rather than gating directly to the island as she had hoped to be able to, she had yet another choice to make. The only towns that she knew had both a portal and a transport gate were Hub and Three Rivers. Neither were places that she enjoyed spending time in but Three Rivers she enjoyed far less. Something about the presence of so many mages, apprentice or otherwise, unnerved her. Her decision made, she used her free transport talisman to gate to Hub.

The placement of the gate network, Wendi discovered, hadn't had much of an impact on the flow of business through the portals so she had to stand and wait in line for almost half an hour for her turn to step into the enormous golden sphere.

"Hot buns," a young woman walked up and down the line of people waiting to use the portal. "Fresh hot buns!"

"Ale," a ruddy man of indeterminate age called out further up the line. "Wet yer throat before yer trip!"

They weren't the only hawkers offering goods to the people waiting in line, a half dozen people walked up and down the length of travelers offering baked goods, beverages, and assorted trinkets. Wendi declined all of their offers but kept a careful eye on her pockets. One fat merchant ahead of her in line wasn't quite as wary, she noticed. From beneath one hawker's cloak, a slim hand reached out and lifted his purse straight off of his belt.

"Where are you headed?" The portal master asked the routine question when it came Wendi's turn in line.

"Tradewinds." Wendi handed the gold tyro to the waiting entrance clerk as she answered. He set it on a small scale to verify its weight before allowing her to pass. She moved to the section of the sphere that would send her to the correct destination and waited for the rest of that trip's passengers to enter.

Travelling by gate was uncomfortable. It made her feel dizzy, nauseated, and a little disoriented by the time she reached the other end of the trip. It wasn't bad, however, and it certainly wasn't uncomfortable enough to make Wendi stop using them. Particularly so because she used them without any need to pay. Where inexpensive was good in her book, free always trumped cheap.

Travelling by portal, on the other hand, made her long for the sweet passage of a gate. Her stomach turned inside out, her head seemed to detach completely from her body, turn completely around, and then reattach once more. Although the trip took only seconds, she could hardly remain standing when she landed. She stumbled and would have fallen had it not been for the tightly-packed group of travelers, all of whom were in a similar state of unwell.

From the loremasters in Tradewinds, she discovered more rumors about the Horn but most of those she was able to dismiss immediately as either fable or the same information she already had. When she discovered on her fourth day in town that she was not the only person looking for it, however, her attention was piqued.

"Seems like everyone wants to get their hands on it these days," one shopkeeper informed her when she asked. "You're the second person this week to ask about it."

Interested, she asked who else had been there to make inquiries. Her excitement faded some as he described the same young man who had been to see Wendi already.

"I heard the Pirate King's been looking for it, too," another shopper added.

"Nah, that can't be true," another pointed out. "The Dark Star killed 'im a while back."

"Well, he was sure 'nuff looking for it before he got dead, then."

Although she tried to find out as much as she could, there wasn't a lot of information to be found. The most common response she found was that the Horn of Ascension was nothing more than a legend; that even if it had once existed, it had been lost to the ages long ago. The only reason she was still willing to believe that the Horn was a real thing was that the loremasters believed it to be real, even if nobody could agree on from where it had come or where it could be found.

Disappointed, she headed back to the portal to wait in the ever-present line again. The only solace to what felt like a thoroughly wasted trip was that she managed to pick up a few things that had just been imported from Sapphire. It'd be nice if there was a gate that headed there, she thought to herself. Only once had she managed to make the trip all the way to Sapphire, which was at the far southern end of the Azul Sea. Her visit there was fantastic, with some of the most amazing and wonderful items available, far more than she could carry in her shop, but plenty to keep her happily shopping and exploring for weeks.

There was a portal that would allow her to travel there again, but using portals to travel quickly grew expensive. At a tyro each direction, she would need to bring a lot more money with her, not to mention an empty wagon to make it worth the trip. While she could travel directly there from Tradewinds, she wouldn't be able to buy much at all, loaded down as she was with all of her purchases.

15

"Looks like you had a good time," Sean grinned at her as he helped her carry her packages into the back room of the shop. "I thought you said you were just getting lamp oil."

"I did get lamp oil," she explained. "It's in the barrel in the back." She had bought almost three times the amount of oil as she had gotten on any of her previous trips to buy it. With how well business had been picking up, she could afford to buy in larger quantities and, considering how quickly they were burning through it, it was very definitely a necessary expense.

"I wasn't able to find out much about the Horn for you," he said as he hauled the heavy barrel from the wagon. "Hethere found out I was in town almost as soon as I got there, so I spent most of my time hiding from her."

"Does that mean you didn't get to see Oree and Hannibal?"

"Oh, no," he smirked. "As soon as I was able to escape her, the three of us went out on Oree's boat to do some fishing."

She snorted. "I thought the point of sending you home was so that you could spend more time with your family."

His smirk faded at her words and his eyes turned serious. "They are family," he said simply. "Those two guys have been like brothers to me for my whole life."

"But what about your mother?" she asked. "Or your father? Did you at least spend a little time with them?"

"Yeah," he sighed. "Or at least, I tried to. But dad was busy in meetings and mayor stuff pretty much the entire time I was there and every time I saw my mother, she had Hethere with her."

This wasn't the first time that Sean had mentioned that he didn't get much of his father's time, which Wendi could understand, given Bart McClannahan's position within the community. She wondered whether that was a cause for his attitude problem. Was he simply trying to get his father's attention? "And you couldn't at least put up with her long enough to spend time with your mother?"

"No, I did. But it's really irritating how the two of them act as though our marriage is already a given. I still don't want to marry her but I can't seem to get her – or mother – to understand that I don't want to." He pulled out another crate from the back of the wagon, a wry smile on his lips. "Honestly, the way things are going, I doubt I'll ever want to get married."

She refrained from saying anything more on the topic. Sean's troubles were personal and she didn't feel as though she could possibly have any valid input on the situation. Rather than making things worse, she decided that the best course of action would be to stay quiet.

"I was able to talk to John," he changed the subject. "He's heard some rumors about the Horn. Not much, really, because he deals in bulk goods and not so much in single items. Especially not expensive and rare items." He chuckled wryly. "He said that there wasn't any money in rare goods. Apparently he hasn't been up here to see your place."

She chuckled as well. "Actually, he has been here. He and Cookie came by a while ago and bought quite a lot." She handed him another package. "Careful with that one."

He took the package gingerly. Having seen her scorch mark riddled lab on more occasions than she cared to count, he had finally learned that there were dangerous things in her collection. "What is it?"

"Hangman's root, thorned valerian and stinging claw," she answered, "and I don't want them to get mixed up.

"He was only here once, and that was a couple months ago. Since then, he's just been sending his agent up to buy and sell on his behalf."

Sean nodded, settling the package of herbs onto the indicated shelf. "That sounds about like him. He's got a lot of people like that who travel to the different towns and make sales for him. But all he'd heard about the Horn of Ascension was that it belonged to an emperor and that it was passed down with the throne somehow."

She twisted her mouth in disappointment. "And nothing else? He travels all over the place so you'd expect him to have better rumors than that." Even she had uncovered more information than what John had come up with and she hadn't traveled nearly as extensively as he had.

"Even if he had heard more rumors, he probably didn't pay them a lot of attention. John believes that the Horn is more legend than fact." He grunted as he lifted one of the casks of whale oil, discovering they were substantially heavier than they appeared. "Beyond that, he thinks that even if the Horn is real, it's a problem for the people of the Dracott Empire, not those of us down here."

It was a fairly commonly held belief, as Wendi had learned. A lot of the people who she had spoken with had expressed similar ideas, often enough that she had even begun to wonder how much of what she was chasing was real and how much was imagination.

Not that she had wondered for long, of course. One thing that Wendi had was an instinct for the unusual. That was one of the reasons that Dragon Trading specialized in the exotic. Every now and again, someone would tell her that she was chasing shadows and that the item of her attention was either nonexistent or not what she expected it to be but she was usually proven to be correct. One of the shelves in her back room was littered with items people believed nonexistent.

Every now and again, of course, she would discover that she had been mistaken but those times were few and far between. Even the time she had spent hunting mirages was time she didn't consider wasted, as she usually managed to uncover something else, often something equally valuable, in the process.

"I think the Horn of Ascension is real," she said after a lengthy pause. When Sean raised a questioning brow, she explained. "Perhaps the original item itself is no longer in existence, I have to accept that possibility but the components to it are out there somewhere." She picked up a small chest and set it on a shelf.

"Unicorns haven't been extinct for so long that bits of them aren't still floating around. While I haven't gotten my hands on unicorn horn, there are still some out there. I know for a fact that the Academy over in Three Rivers has some in its artifacts room." And as rare and closely guarded as garnets were, some had managed to escape the Dracott Empire, so there was a chance that she could find some of them as well.

She still wasn't positive about the history of the legendary Horn that had led her to start her search in the first place. It seemed like a strange thing to have as a part of the coronation regalia but she knew that there were stranger things out there. The royal family of the Inland Empire, for example, supposedly had a magical robe that the succeeding emperor wore during his crowning ceremony, said to transfer all of the secret knowledge of the previous monarchs. At the death of the leader of the Barberry Empire, all of the clan leaders gathered together for a secret ceremony where a set of special stones determined which was most worthy of the ascension. If both of those empires could have strange relics and unusual requirements, why couldn't the Dracott Empire have some of their own?

The more she thought about it, the more certain Wendi became that the Horn existed, exactly as the legends said it did. And if so many people were looking for it, then it would stand to reason that it had been stolen or taken from the empire in some manner. She didn't care how or why it had been taken and she cared even less who had it. All she knew was that she wanted to see it, to hold it, at least once in her lifetime.

16

Ignus lizards had to be the single most frustrating creatures that Wendi had ever worked with. They refused to do what they were supposed to do, blew up over absolutely nothing and just plain took up time and effort that would have been better spent elsewhere. All of those things were just made worse by the fact that the creatures she was fighting with weren't even alive.

The glands that she had removed from the lizards she and Jaegar killed in the Fusite Desert simply refused to behave. At first, she had wondered if she had simply let the glands sit for too long but even after making an overnight trip to gather more hadn't helped.

They were just plain unstable.

As she put out yet another fire, the tenth one she had set in her lab over the two weeks since getting fresh specimens, she wondered if perhaps it was time to put them away and focus on something else for a while. For the moment, however, she needed to get some fresh air while the smoke cleared out of her lab. She plucked her cloak from its hook and headed for the stairs.

"There you are," Sean spotted her as she wove through the store-room, eyeing barrels and casks to see how much stock they contained and making a list of the items they were low on. "I've got the back lot cleared out for more of the menagerie."

"Good," she made a small mark on a crate with her chalk. The small round mirrors that she had picked up in Ankh-Ra were selling well. She should probably go back to get more soon.

"What do you want me working on next?"

Before Wendi could think of another task for him, Crucian walked into the room. "Your mother's lookin' for you," he said when he spotted Sean.

Sean uttered an epithet and ducked behind another row of stock. "She didn't follow you in here, did she?"

Wendi uttered an oath of her own and grabbed him by an arm. "It's your mother. The least you can do is go see her."

"But you don't understand," he complained as she pulled him out of the room. "She's got Hethere with her again."

"So?" Wendi didn't slow down. "She's still your mother, no matter who she brought with her. The least you can do is be polite." Reaching the door that led to the shop, she looked over at Crucian. "Where are they?"

"In the tavern," he supplied, watching them with obvious amusement.

Wendi nodded her thanks to him and pulled a loudly complaining Sean out through the shop and across the courtyard toward the tavern. To his credit, he didn't put up much physical resistance despite his argument. Had he really dug in his heels, she was sure there was no way she would be able to drag him anywhere. Through the windows, she could see Hethere and an older, striking woman who must have been Sean's mother. "Pretend you have some manners," she said as she thrust him in through the door.

His mother looked over at her in surprise at the exchange but Hethere's smile was more of a sneer than anything else. The young woman dismissed Wendi as soon as she let go of Sean and stepped lightly over to embrace him. As she wrapped her arms around the taller man, Hethere sent Wendi a look that was part challenge and part condescension.

Wendi didn't stop to consider why the girl seemed to believe that it was Wendi's fault that Sean didn't want to see her. It wasn't any of her business and frankly, she didn't care what the obnoxious girl thought. Each time she met Hethere, she irritated her even more. Of course today was no exception.

Ignoring the small family and leaving them to their supper, she headed back to her lab. The smoke should have cleared out by then, at least she hoped it had, and there were about a dozen things that she needed to make more of if she didn't want to run completely out. Sales of her chewing gums had increased rapidly and she was constantly running out, which meant that there was a batch curing on her drying racks all the time. She just hoped that the smoke hadn't caused an odd flavor in this batch.

After setting another vat of snake venom to distill, she turned to look through her ingredients, debating on creating another flavor of gum. But what? She pulled down a bottle of water from the geyser at the Adlep Oasis and considered it thoughtfully for a moment before returning it to the shelf. If she tried using it, she was far more likely to create a gum that caused excessive drooling rather than anything else.

"As entertaining as that would be," she mused to herself, "I can't imagine many people will want to buy them."

Her eyes ran over a tightly-capped jar of powdered pixie wings but she dismissed it immediately. Though most people thought pixie dust only caused a fit of giggles and a few crazy moments, prolonged exposure caused instability and the inability to discern between the real world and the chronic hallucinations the dust caused.

She dug through bottles of blessed water, jars of dirt from the mausoleum at Sorrel, dried Bleeding-Heart root, and a small box of Naga scales. None of them had properties that she thought would be good to add to her gum. Finally, she picked up a jar of spores from the Gaplan mushroom and considered its contents.

Gaplan mushrooms weren't very rare, growing almost everywhere in the Powne Swamp, but they caused temporary disorientation, an intense sensation of weightlessness, and an almost unbelievable urge to laugh. The effects didn't last very long and, as long as she only added a small amount of the spores, it should make the gum a source of amusement. The mushrooms themselves, when found growing freely, caused people to get lost in the swamp, so disoriented that they never made their way back out again. Wendi had discovered through her research and repeated inflictions on Crucian that two or three pinches of the spores should be safe for regular use.

"I'll need to find something to cover the flavor," she muttered to herself. "Most people don't like musky flavors in their sweets. But this will do nicely.

"Now... what flavor seems like it would go well with euphoria?" she asked herself as she walked back up to the storeroom. "Wild cherry? Huckleberry? Ginger?"

She continued muttering to herself as she walked down the aisles, considering all of the different flavors that she could add to the gum. Some of them weren't strong enough to cover the taste of the bitter mushrooms and some just seemed like a bad idea. As she walked up the next aisle, however, she almost tripped across Sean.

He was sitting on a barrel, his boots resting on the shelf across from him and his head leaned back against a soft package of fleece. His eyes were closed but he wasn't asleep, she could tell by his breathing. "What do you think you're doing?" she demanded as she stopped next to him.

"Taking a break," he explained without opening his eyes.

"Phemie said she sent you to organize the cases of mead," she snapped. "In case you hadn't noticed, the mead's in the next room."

"Oh, I know," he finally opened his eyes and looked at her, dropping his boots to the floor with a solid-sounding thump. Stretching as he moved, he rose to his full height and stood looking down at her. "But there wasn't a lot of it to organize."

She looked at him, dumbfounded. While he had been back at the Keep, he had gotten better about not taking breaks every time she turned around, so this sudden reversion back to his old behavior was surprising. "What's going on with you?" she demanded, equally confused and annoyed at the change. "Are you trying to get sent back home so you can marry your girl? Because you know you're free to leave at any time."

His eyes darkened as he stepped closer to her. A year before, she would have been intimidated but those days were long past. She stood her ground and glared right back up at him.

"I think you're just jealous," he said. "I have people lining up to be with me but you're all alone in this little shop and locked away in your lab."

She blinked at him, stunned. He had said some nasty things to her before but their relationship had grown closer to friendship lately, so this assault had come completely out of nowhere. She would have slapped him but he caught her hand easily. "Just because you're lonely and miserable, you seem to think that everyone else around you needs to be miserable, too." He stepped even closer as he spoke, whether it was to try again to intimidate her or to make it harder for her to slap him, she wasn't sure.

"You're the miserable one," she retorted. "Hiding away from your friends and family because you're scared of a little girl. It's amazing that she's even willing to be seen with you, let alone agree to marry you." She didn't try to pull her hand back away from him, but she didn't try to slap him with her other one, either.

"If I was in your position, I would thank the gods you're a McClannahan. That name's about the only thing that would get a woman to spend time with you willingly."

The pair of them continued to toss insults at each other, voices rising and anger building with each barb. Before she knew what was happening, she was pressed back against one of the shelves, the corner of a box digging painfully into her shoulder but she didn't care. He still held her hand in one of his but the other was tangled in her hair as he ravaged her mouth with his own, his body pressed tightly against hers. Her hands, in return, were wrapped around him, her fingers digging into his shoulders and kissing him back just as forcefully.

The sound of someone quietly laughing nearby brought her back to reality. When she opened her eyes, she discovered that Crucian was standing next to them, reaching over both their heads to lift down a case of bird-of-paradise quills. "Don't stop on my account," he sniggered as he turned to walk away.

Mortified, Wendi pushed Sean away, shoving him into the rack behind him. "You need to get back to work," she said breathlessly. Almost running in her haste, she snapped up a jar of wild cherry preserves on her way back down to her lab. Even though she still wasn't certain that was the best flavor to use, she wasn't interested in spending any more time in the storeroom at that moment. It would just have to do.

What in all the hells had that been about?

"I mean seriously," Phemie accosted Wendi in her lab a couple hours later. "You don't even like the man. What is going on?"

"I don't know," Wendi answered through gritted teeth.

"You must have some idea," she pressed. "Even poor, simple Crucian was able to tell me what you were up to." She googled her eyes knowingly at her friend. "Sounded like things were getting pretty steamy back there, too."

"He was slacking off again so I yelled at him a little bit, nothing different from what's happened before."

"You mean this has happened before?" Phemie's eyes lit up with interest. "Come on, I want to hear all the juicy details."

"No," she waved her friend down. She should have known Crucian would mention to Phemie what he had seen. There was going to be absolutely no living this down now, she knew. "That's not what I meant. The yelling at each other and arguing, that's happened lots of times before." Although not so much recently, for a while fighting had practically been their favorite pastime, so far as anyone else could tell.

"Yeah, but the yelling never ended in heavy breathing before, at least not so far as I knew." Phemie looked thoughtful for a moment before asking, "Did he use a philter on you?"

Wendi snorted derisively at the idea. "Are you kidding me? He's already doing his best to avoid one woman. Why would he go out of his way to attract another one?" She leveled her black eyes at her friend. "Particularly one like me," she added much more quietly.

"Did you use one on him?" When Wendi's eyes widened, appalled, the witch raised her hands defensively. "Don't get mad, I think it's good to see you spending some time with a man for a change." She looked around the lab and sniffed. "You spend far too much time down here, locked up with your experiments. Been saying for a while that you needed something to bring you up out of here more often.

"Besides, Sean's pretty good looking." Phemie grinned conspiratorially at her. "But I'm assuming you noticed that already."

Wendi made as if she was going to throw a bottle of scarab carapaces at her and Phemie dodged, giggling madly. "If you don't want him," she added as she ducked out the door, "can I have him?"

Wendi tried to push what had happened from her mind but unless she was using all of her energy to focus on the task at hand, her mind kept drifting back to how good it had felt to have Sean's lips pressed to hers, to feel the smooth muscle of his shoulders beneath her fingers, to...

"Get a grip," she chided herself, shaking her head to derail where her train of thoughts had been heading. "You're not some young, foolish twit." She slammed the bottle of scarab carapaces back onto the shelf where they belonged. She knew that she had taken them down for a reason but she couldn't remember what she had been intending to do with them.

"It was a mistake," she reminded herself, "And it won't happen again."

17

Wendi spent the next few days avoiding Sean as much as she could, determined not to put either of them into a position where a repeat performance could be had. When there was work that she needed him to do, she sent Jaegar or Crucian to inform him.

She would have sent Phemie but the witch still had a gleam in her eye that Wendi knew meant she was up to no good. Twice, she caught her friend trying to slip an attraction philter into her pocket. Wendi just hoped that she hadn't tried to do the same thing with Sean.

It seemed as though Sean reciprocated her unwillingness to spend any more time together than necessary. He stayed out of sight, cleaning out the stables and working to put more of the Keep's buildings back into working order. He still didn't work anywhere near as quickly as Oree or Hannibal had but Wendi wasn't in a mood to argue about it.

Not once did he come looking for her, either in her rooms or downstairs in her lab and she was fine with that. She still wasn't sure what had happened between them in the storeroom but she was sure it didn't need to happen again.

"He's a selfish prat," she explained to her empty lab. "He's nothing like what I would look for in a man – not that I've been actually looking." She sprinkled a few more grains of dried cherry into her latest mixture wondering, not for the first time, why she felt the need to defend herself to an empty room.

"Besides, it's only a matter of time before he gets fed up with life here and moves back to Hoem to marry *Hethere*," she said, stretching the name so that it was barely recognizable, "and make beautiful, red-haired, self-centered babies with her."

"Besides," she reminded herself once again an hour and a half of failed experimentation later, "you have more important things to worry about instead of that jerk." Her eyes rose to meet the stack of missing persons reports she had collected and she made a decision. She had spent enough time wallowing. It was time to step up her search.

"Phemie," she stopped her friend at the close of business. "Would you start checking with some of the adventuring parties and merchants that stop in at the shop to see if any of them have heard about missing person reports from about five years ago?"

"I suppose so," she looked at her friend curiously. "Anything in particular I'm looking for?"

Wendi shrugged. "Still not sure myself. Female, late teens to early twenties. Other than that, I have no idea." She knew it was a long time ago and the odds of finding anything were slim but it was worth a shot. The worst she could find was nothing and she had found plenty of that already.

In the meantime, she had plans to make. There was still a long list of places where she had not yet made inquiries and the longer she put it off, the less information she would be able to get. She packed enough supplies for a long journey and headed for the gate.

Her request had been over two weeks before and so far, Phemie had managed to turn up even more of the absolutely nothing Wendi was already fully stocked on. After spending a small fortune on portal fees, travelling to everywhere that she could have conceivably been from, she had turned up no new information at all.

But at least she had another stack of useless missing person fliers. That was more than she'd previously had.

"Maybe I was from somewhere outside the Inland Empire," she mused to herself. Although she still firmly believed that the Inland Empire had been her home, she had to at least consider the possibility that she was mistaken.

"Or maybe I was missing for more than five years." The likelihood that she had been gone for longer than just the time she had memories as Wendi was distinct. Just because her knowledge only went back five years, that didn't mean that she hadn't been gone from her previous life for much longer than that. "How long have I really been gone for?"

There was a third option, one that was both more likely and less pleasant to consider than any of the others she had come up with. Perhaps the reason that nobody had reported her missing was simply because nobody had cared.

On almost any street of any town of any empire, children lived and died with nobody to care for them. Those children lived anonymously and when one of them disappeared, it was hardly newsworthy. Nobody bothered reporting the disappearance of a street urchin or any of the other multitude of undesirable people in their towns. Wendi suspected, as much as she didn't want to admit it, that she could have been one of these unwanted children, unnoticed and forgotten.

"No," she denied even as the horrifying thoughts traveled through her head. "I wasn't. I couldn't have been."

The earliest memories she had were from a small farming village just past Wilee. She had woken in a field, soon falling into a panic because she had no clue where she was or how she had gotten there. Tall stalks of corn surrounded her and the field was so large that she couldn't see anything beyond it. There were no trails winding through the field, no indication of how she had gotten there in the first place.

She had stumbled through the field for hours and she had never forgotten the feeling of despair as she had wandered, lost and alone. Finally she came close enough to the edge of the corn field to discover a small village in the distance and she had taken off at a run, ecstatic to see civilization at last. Maybe someone in the village could tell her where she was, she had hoped. Maybe someone could even tell her how she had gotten there.

Her ecstasy didn't last long. As soon as she set foot inside the town, people began to stare, covering their children and making signs of warding against her. Some of the more frightened villagers ran in fear at just the sight of her and she couldn't understand why they were so afraid. She wondered if she was covered in blood or some other frightening substance but she had been dressed in a simple brown travelling robe and boots. Even if she had been covered in blood, it would have hardly shown against the rough cloth.

Walking past a storefront, still in search of someone who was willing to help her, she spotted a fearsome creature looking out through the glass at her. It looked like a human, more or less, but with a grossly disfigured face and empty, soulless eye sockets. She fell back in fear at the sight.

Only then did she realize she was looking at a reflection of herself.

The scar had been fresh then, an angry red clump of torn flesh on the side of her face. "What is that?" she asked. Reaching up to touch it, she pulled her fingers back immediately as a shock of pain traveled from her cheek through her entire body at the contact. As the pain slowly subsided, she recognized that she had been feeling its dull, throbbing ache since waking up.

Her eyes, however, were what truly frightened her. Her sockets were not empty, as they had appeared at first glance but the orbs inside them were such a deep, matte black that they reflected absolutely no light.

It was no wonder they had called her a demon.

She looked like one.

She left the small town as quickly as she could, running for her life to escape the braver townsfolk who had banded together to kill the demon. Armed with axes, pitchforks and even sharpened pikes made of fence posts, they chased her, mistakenly believing that they were saving their town from certain doom.

On her own, a situation she soon realized would be her status for the rest of her miserable existence, she wandered the forests and glens, staying out of sight of any who may try to harm her. She killed small game for food and defended herself against larger predators who had believed her to be food. Survival was all that she thought about. Any time spent on feeling lonely and sorry for herself was time wasted.

It was after such a fight, where she had been beset by a small pack of wild, territorial firehounds that she met Phemie. The young witch had been out gathering components and had calmly approached Wendi after she killed two of the creatures and had driven the last one off.

"Are you going to use both of those?" she had asked her.

Wendi looked up at her in surprise. "I guess I'm going to eat one," she answered hesitantly. At any moment, she knew, the woman would run screaming.

Phemie looked, directly and unflinchingly, into her eyes, the first time in Wendi's memory that anyone had done so. "Then you'll need some help cooking it. Need a hand starting a fire?"

They had shared the meal that night, the first of many. Over that single, simple meal, Wendi received the human companionship that she had been missing for as long as she could remember, short as that amount of time may have been, and the two of them had become fast friends.

Wendi began accompanying Phemie when she went out hunting for components. After a few months, when they were going after bigger and bigger game, Phemie began bringing Crucian and then Jaegar along on the hunts. Just like Phemie, neither of the men seemed to notice Wendi's unusual features. Wendi had never been sure whether the witch had warned them before bringing them out to meet her or whether they simply hadn't noticed. Wendi was a part of a group now and that was all that mattered.

When they needed money or supplies, it had been Phemie to enter the towns as they passed, buying or selling as needed. She had been the one to buy Wendi her first long-hooded cloak so that she could accompany the witch into towns without the reactions of the towns-people driving her back out again. For the most part, Wendi still wasn't comfortable dealing with people, so she had only gone with Phemie when there had been more items to buy or sell than Phemie could carry on her own.

She got used to the stares people gave her as she passed but as long as nobody was screaming "demon," she didn't care. They may have looked at her oddly because she covered her face with a hood but at least they weren't screaming in terror. Even better, they weren't organizing hunting parties to try and kill her.

Wendi had paid attention as Phemie mixed and brewed her herbs and other components into spells and potions. Phemie had encouraged her to try some spellwork herself but Wendi had never been able to achieve the same effects the witch had, even with the simplest of spells. A good mixture for Wendi was one that simply didn't work. A bad one was one that exploded or created an unwanted, unexpected result.

One evening, using some of the leftover bits that Phemie hadn't wanted, Wendi discovered how to make a batch of slimy, slippery goo. The goo had been completely useless, good for nothing whatsoever but Wendi had found her passion. While Phemie hunted for components for use in her magic, Wendi hunted for ingredients with unusual properties, fascinated by what she was discovering. Soon, she had a small collection of recipes that she had created and fine-tuned, hers and hers alone.

When Wendi stumbled across Dragon Keep, it seemed to have been sent by the gods. It had been abandoned years before and had fallen into severe disrepair. Old, crumbling and beset by beasts of all kinds it may have been but Wendi fell in love with it immediately. It had taken over a year before she had gathered together enough tyros to purchase it but it had been worth every single one.

The closest town to the Keep was Landor and the next closest after that was Three Rivers. Nobody from either town would make the trip up to Dragon Keep to bother her. It was away from everyone, and that was all that mattered.

She was safe there.

But she still had questions.

18

Barely paying attention to what she was doing, Wendi made a vat of her slippery goo. She had refined the recipe over the years so now her mixture would stay slippery for just over an hour before thickening and solidifying. After three hours, the entire mess could be picked up in one giant sheet.

There was no reason to check her notes, she had the formula embedded in her memory so deeply that she could do it in her sleep if she needed to. Of course, she still had it written down, just in case something happened and her memories were lost again.

That possibility was the primary reason why she had everything written down. Stacks of notes, scrolls, and all sorts of papers were neatly stored on the shelves of her laboratory, detailing everything that she had uncovered. A leather-bound journal rested at the edge of her bench, ready for her to make the day's entry. She detailed the events of each day, recording for herself everything that had happened, no matter how inconsequential those events may seem. If she ever lost her memories again, at least she wouldn't have to start over from nothing.

Some adventurers had discovered the substance soon after the shop had opened and they touted it as the best stuff they had ever used for trapping small animals and other creatures. Apparently, a single vial of her goo could create a yards-wide area of terrain that nothing could pass through easily.

Other people used it as a cleaning solution and Wendi had used it for that purpose herself on a couple of occasions. As the goo solidified, it picked up dust, grime, and all manner of dirt, trapping it inside so that an entire room could be made completely clean just by pouring a vial of the liquid over it. Because of the hazardous nature of the components she worked with, it had proven invaluable for cleaning up spilled acids, flammable substances and all manner of other problematic ingredients that landed on the floor.

While the thick mixture gurgled over the low flame, she pulled out a handful of other items that she had purchased at different shops the last time she had gone out on her rounds. She was always interested in discovering what other alchemists were working on. Sometimes, she would simply go back to the store where she had made the original purchase after discovering how their concoctions worked but others interested her more and she had to replicate them.

She refused to steal the ideas and recipes of other alchemists, however, so after she discovered how their creations did what they did, she spent hours – sometimes days – working on them and changing them to make them different from the original. Perhaps her developments weren't always better, she realized, but they were always different.

One of the more unusual concoctions she had picked up was a simple vial of liquid. As it poured out, however, it turned into a thick, secure rope-like substance. "Must be a reaction to the air," she muttered to herself as she examined the fluid through the clear vial. "Kind of like how the Ignus lizards' glands do."

With a few modifications, she thought, she might be able to make a similar item out of her slippery goo. Just like the formula she had purchased, her goo started as a liquid and became solid. There were just a few steps in the middle of the process that would need to change. The vat that she already had brewing would continue to develop as goo to be sold in the shop but she pulled out more of the ingredients to make another batch. Some of the ingredients stayed on her bench but others went back onto their shelves. They wouldn't be used in this mixture. Now, she just needed to figure out what else to add to it.

While she was perusing her shelves, looking for the right ingredients to add, she heard a commotion coming from upstairs. The door to her lab was open to let fresh air in, as brewing her goo smelled terrible and the less of its fumes she had to breathe, the better. She expected the commotion to end shortly after it began, that was one of Crucian and Jaegar's primary functions at the Keep, but the sounds continued. If anything, she realized, they were growing louder.

Irritated at the interruption but concerned over the continued noises from overhead, she checked the flame on her burner before grabbing her cloak and heading for the stairs.

"Don't go out there," Crucian grabbed her as soon as she reached the top of the stairs. "There's bad people looking for you."

A chill of fear ran down Wendi's spine at his words. "Who?"

"Don't know,' he replied. "They just want you and they're making a mess to find you."

Confused, scared, and angry, she jogged down the short hall that led to the shop.

Armed men and women were everywhere she could see. They filled her courtyard, swarmed through her shops and even as she watched, more of them continued flooding in through the gate. Almost everyone she saw was armed with cutlasses and sabers and many of them were menacing her customers. Fires had been set everywhere, with more fires being set as she surveyed the scene. Other pirates, for that was all they could have been, were overturning carts and dumping the wares that her merchants had either brought in to sell or had just purchased but hadn't been able to leave with before the attack.

This was precisely why she hadn't been interested in opening trade too close to the Pirate Run. They were simply too dangerous, too un-predictable for her tastes. Now it appeared that her lack of interest in their business had offended them somehow.

As she strode into the courtyard, her eyes fell on a familiar figure. The young man who had come to the keep to inquire about his missing family heirloom, a story that Wendi had recognized as false immedi-ately, stood in the middle of the chaos, calmly watching Dragon Keep burn. He turned slightly and, noticing her arrival, smiled broadly and turned to walk towards her, raising a hand in greeting as though he was making a social visit. Unlike the mass of pirates swarming the keep, he was apparently unarmed.

"I know you have it," he said as he approached. "After all, you were the one to get it for me in the first place so it only makes sense that you would have gotten it for me again."

"What are you talking about?" she asked coldly. Her initial dislike of the man had grown into something stronger, something fiercer. Hate was not a strong enough description for what she was feeling but it was the strongest word she could come up with at that moment. Disgust came a close second, followed by revulsion.

"The Horn of Ascension, of course. You and I both know the Dark Star sold it out from under me and this is the only place in the Inland Sea where she could have sold it. Now, all you have to do is hand it over like a good girl and all will be forgiven." His smile grew cold and his eyes grew hard as he spoke.

She didn't bother answering him. She had no idea what he was talking about but it didn't matter. The son of a rabid donkey had set fire to her keep, her refuge from the fear and chaos of the world, the one place in this entire godsforsaken land that she could feel safe and she was going to make sure he regretted it. While he continued to speak, she stepped around him and walked, calmly and deliberately, toward the gate. His words held no meaning to her, particularly since he wasn't saying anything that made sense, so there was no reason for her to hear him out. Pirates had ceased passing through the transport gate, so while it was silent, she seized the opportunity to reach out and pluck the capstone from the top.

Not that it would have mattered, of course. There could have been a person halfway through the gate and she wouldn't have hesitated to dismantle it.

If they thought this was going to be an easy assault, they had attacked the wrong keep.

"Of course, you'll have to come with me," she heard him say from behind her. "Your services will likely be needed in the near future."

She dropped the stone into the pocket of her cloak, relieved that at least the flow of pirates had stopped flooding into her home. She would worry about what that meant for business later.

It also meant, she thought as she turned to face the still-smiling sociopath, no pirates would be leaving through her gate, either.

"You come into my keep," she said furiously as she stepped toward him. "Acting like you own the place, setting fire to everything you see, and then you dare to give orders to me?" She advanced slowly, giving voice to her rage as she moved. "Not only have I not found this Horn you're seeking but I have no intention whatsoever of going anywhere with you.

"However, as you obviously seem to think you know something about me, I think I have a few questions for you."

Pirates moved closer, trying to surround her as she approached their leader. They pressed tighter and she calmly lifted her hood away from her face and leveled her obsidian eyes at them.

Almost as one, the pirates fell away from her in fear. The knife-edged resignation of what she was doing twisted in her chest but she forcibly brushed it aside. This was the first time she had intentionally used her appearance to cause fear in another person but there was too much at stake. The lives of her employees and her guests – not to mention her own life – were far too valuable to let the pirates continue to rampage unchecked, terrorizing her home. She would deal with the aftermath from anyone else who saw her later, once everything had calmed down again.

Of all the pirates, only their leader seemed unaffected by her visage. His smile, never faltering, twisted into a cruel sneer. "You don't frighten me," he said. "I already locked away all of your power.

"If you don't do exactly as I tell you to, you'll never have another chance to get it back."

19

Trying to escape, most of the invading pirates gathered at the gate through which they had entered the keep, trying to use it to travel back to whatever pit they had come from. In their frenzy to attack, it appeared that none of them had noticed that Wendi had broken it. Their fear turned to terror as they realized that it wouldn't work and they were trapped.

Their leader, on the other hand, continued to stand calmly in the middle of Wendi's courtyard, his mouth twisted in a vile caricature of pleasure. His eyes still hadn't left Wendi's and the fear that she had hoped to instill in him, as well as his men, didn't seem to be working.

"Your men are free to go," she explained calmly. "They leave their weapons here and leave by the road. Nobody uses the gate again until I say so."

Slowly, the man pulled a long, thin chain from beneath his tunic and held it up for her to see. It was a bright, polished chain that she initially believed to be silver but it wasn't quite bright enough. Instead, she realized it was platinum – one of the rarest and therefore most expensive metals in all the land. From the end a tiny, black skull-shaped pendant dangled.

Something about the necklace, particularly the pendant it held, seemed familiar but she couldn't quite recognize either. It felt like something that she had seen from before her memories started, or perhaps during the foggy first handful of days of her new life. She wasn't positive that was where she had encountered them, it just seemed that way. Never before had she felt such an intense and immediate connection with any item and she wasn't sure she liked the feeling.

Before she could say anything, while her attention was still riveted on the macabre jewelry, an arrow flew from somewhere behind her. It soared through the air a hands-breadth from her head and slammed into the man's shoulder. A second arrow followed the first, missing him but only barely.

The pirate leader looked down at the arrow in his shoulder, his face growing pale. He raised his eyes to meet hers, murder clearly expressed in them and then looked behind her in the direction from which the pair of arrows had come. "Men," he called out in a powerful voice, one that was far more forceful than what his small form should have been able to project. "We're leaving." He waved with his good arm to the pirates who were still gathered around the transport gate. As soon as he had their attention, he turned and led them out through the front gate of the keep and onto the road that led to Three Rivers. The small handful of merchants who were near the front gates, now released from harassment by the pirates, backed away to let them pass.

The pirates withdrew from each corner of the keep, setting a few small fires as they moved. As the pirates and their wounded leader left, Wendi ran into the throng of armed men in an attempt to reach the man with the mysterious skull-shaped necklace but she was knocked aside by the horde. She landed painfully on the ground, scraping her elbow in the fall but that was the least of her concerns.

That man knew who she was. His words had made that singular fact abundantly clear. He knew something about her and if she couldn't figure out a way to get him to tell her what it was while he was still within her reach, she might lose the opportunity to ever find out.

"Wait," she called out after him. "What was that? What do you know?"

Her calls fell on deaf ears. If he heard anything of what she had asked, he gave absolutely no indication. Followed by his pirate troops, he strode out through the gate and disappeared down the road.

Wendi pushed herself back to her feet, tugging her hood over her eyes as more a matter of habit than anything else, to no avail. By the time she regained her feet, the pirate leader was completely surrounded by his men and well beyond the gates of Dragon Keep.

She stared after him in shock as he left, her heartbeat thundering in her ears. That was the closest she had ever been to the secrets she had so long been seeking and he had just walked away, revealing nothing. All because someone had shot him. Remembering that the arrows had come from behind her, she whirled around to see from whom it had come.

"What do you think you're doing?" she demanded furiously as Sean walked calmly toward her, bow in hand.

"Saving your life," he retorted. "You're welcome."

"Saving nothing," she howled at him. "That was the best chance I've ever come across to find the information he had and you ruined it!"

Confusion spread over Sean's face. "What are you talking about?"

"That man knows something about me, and now he's gone." She all but sobbed the last as she stormed past him and into the keep. People stared at her as she passed, but she didn't care.

Sean grabbed her just inside the door, where he finally managed to catch up with her. "That guy was going to kill you," he protested. "If I hadn't shot him, he would have either killed you on the spot or kidnapped you off somewhere else to kill you."

"You don't know that," she said as she yanked her arm from his grasp. She glared up at him, tears streaming from her eyes but she didn't care. Her whole body was shaking from a combination of fury from the attack, fear from the unknown and frustration from having lost the best lead she had ever found to her own history. "He knew something about me, something important, and you drove him away before I could find out anything at all."

"What is wrong with you?" he demanded. "I saved your life and you're mad at me for it? You should be mad at that guy, not at me."

"I never asked to be saved," she snapped in return. "And I especially never asked to be saved by an arrogant ass like you!"

She knew she wasn't making much sense. There was no reason for Sean to understand what had just happened. She was angry, she was frustrated, and most of all she was worried that she had no further recourse to get the information from the pirates and their leader now that they had left. There was no reason for her to take her ire out on Sean but she couldn't help herself. The emotions, feelings that she had been struggling against for years, had finally bubbled to the surface, no longer contained beneath her deliberately cool exterior, and she had no idea how to stop them.

He grabbed her again as she tried to leave, pulling her tightly against him and wrapping both of his arms around her. Her breath caught in her throat as he leaned down and, far more gently than she would have expected, pressed his lips to her own. "I was worried about you," he said, his lips barely moving as he kissed her. "Just let me worry about you once in a while, would you?"

20

Years before, Wendi had started making sketches of the items she worked with, items that may or may not have had some interesting properties. At first, those sketches had been truly poor renderings, bad enough that she had made replacement drawings once her skill began to improve. Every item in her lab, from the smallest mermaid scale to the large dried squid tentacle, had a meticulous drawing in one of her books.

Initially, the drawings had been for her to differentiate among some of the items Phemie taught her about but then she had continued because she feared losing her memories again and even her notes, detailed as they were, wouldn't tell her the difference between regular anise and star anise unless she had pictures of both of them. Now, she had scrolls upon scrolls, detailed sketches of the different materials she had gathered and the important properties of each.

Those skills at sketching plants and animals from memory were being thoroughly tested as she put quill to parchment, trying to create an accurate representation of the skull pendant the pirate leader had been wearing. She had started and re-started the drawing so many times that pieces of discarded parchment littered her floor. Finally, however, it looked like she had a reasonable facsimile.

She had no idea what the pendant was or why it was important. She didn't know if the rest of the necklace, the platinum chain to which the pendant had been attached, was important as well but she added it to her sketch just to be sure. She figured that it was better to add it and discover later that it was unnecessary than to not add it and find that it was a crucial piece of the puzzle.

When she was finished with the drawing, she carried it upstairs, careful to pull her hood down over her eyes once more. She knew that most of her customers had already seen enough to know she was strange but there was no reason to flaunt it and any who had not seen her display in the courtyard didn't need the trauma now. She posted the image on the shop's notice board and added a request for any information about the item itself or its whereabouts.

As she looked around, she was pleased to discover that all of the fires that had been set by the invading pirates had been put out. The damage from the flames hadn't been as extensive as she had initially thought it to be but there were a handful of places where she could see that repair work would be needed.

"Could you ask Crucian to repair the burned section of the inn when he gets a chance?" she asked Phemie as she finished posting her notice.

"Thanks," Wendi said when she agreed. "And thanks for taking care of the rest of the people here." She glanced around the shop, amazed to discover that people were acting much more calmly than she had expected. "Soothing tonics?"

"Of a sort," Phemie giggled. "Everyone got a free sample of your new firebrandy. A few of them liked it so much they're still over in the tavern drinking."

Wendi smiled at her friend. Phemie was remarkably astute about what would calm and soothe people. A jug or three of firebrandy was more than adequate compensation for the trouble.

And trouble there would be, she was sure. One of the first things Wendi had tried doing after all of the pirates had left had been to replace the capstone that she had taken from the transportation gate. She had known it would be futile but she had to try. Magical items, no matter what type they were, couldn't just be taken apart and then reassembled later without the proper sequence of spells. In the morning, she would head down to Three Rivers and see how much Analisse and her associates would charge her to repair it.

She glanced around the courtyard, but didn't see Sean anywhere. His absence didn't bother her very much. After the pointless fight she had picked with him earlier, she wasn't surprised that he was making himself scarce. She would just have to remember to apologize to him when he finished with whatever he was doing. Hopefully her intended apology wouldn't turn into another argument. She was tired of fighting.

When suppertime came and went with still no sign of him, however, she began to get concerned. When darkness fell and he had still not been seen, Wendi became worried. She began to ask her employees if any of them knew where he was. To her dismay, she discovered that he had left shortly after the pirates were gone.

"I don't know," Phemie said gently when Wendi asked if she knew where he had gone. "He didn't tell anyone where he was headed or when he'd be back." At Wendi's morose expression, she tried to reassure her. "He will be back." She laid a hand on Wendi's arm. "After all, this was hardly the first fight you two have had.

"I hadn't realized that he left at the same time as you disappeared into your lab," she added as Wendi turned to leave. "Kind of disappointing, really."

"Why is that disappointing?"

The small witch shrugged. "After the way you two have been ending your quarrels as of late, I had hoped you'd finally come to your senses and taken him to your bed."

At breakfast the next morning, there was still no sign of Sean. Disappointed but not angry at his absence, Wendi decided it was high time she started taking care of the merchants who had become trapped at the keep when she broke the transport gate. The closest functioning gate was at Landor and she believed that was where she needed to escort her guests so that they could get back to their homes. At the same time, she could use the gate from Landor to go to Three Rivers and find Analisse.

"If I can have your attention," she called out to everyone who was having breakfast in the tavern. "As most of you know, our transport gate is no longer functioning. The closest working gate to here is half a day away in Landor. I am willing to accompany you to Landor to make sure that you all arrive safely so that you can use their gate and I will send word to all of you once ours is functioning again."

A general murmur of agreement echoed through the building at her proclamation but it was cut short by a second announcement, spoken by a strong masculine voice directly behind her. "Or you could just wait for a few hours longer and we'll have the gate here up and running for you."

She spun around at the sound of Sean's voice, certain that she had misidentified its source. To her amazement, he stood only inches away from her, his cocky grin firmly in place. Behind him, she could see Analisse and Remy, one of her partners.

"I already told them what happened with your gate," Sean explained in response to her astonished, confused expression.

"We think we know how to make the capstone movable," Remy added. "In fact, we're even considering making it a feature on all of them, just in case something like this happens again."

The murmuring behind her became more excited as the merchants caught what was said. A few of them who had risen to prepare their wagons for the overland journey settled back down again, ordering more food and drinks.

The repairs to the gate took a bit longer than expected, considering the modifications Remy had to put into place so that the stone could be removed without crashing all of the magic again. By the time he and Analisse had the gate operational, it was almost suppertime and most of the traders were eager to leave before they had to purchase rooms at the inn for another night at the Keep.

Wendi brought the mages into the tavern and offered them supper and drinks in addition to payment for their assistance. Both of them agreed gratefully, so she had meals brought out for them immediately. While they were eating, Remy stopped with his spoon halfway to his mouth, staring in shock. "Why would you actually be looking for one of those?" he asked.

"What?" Wendi looked to see what he was so startled by. "What are you talking about?"

"The trapping stone," he explained, pointing to the sketch of the necklace the pirate had been wearing. She had made a couple more copies of the sketch and placed them in the tavern and the inn, just to ensure that more people saw them. Apparently it had worked.

"What's a trapping stone?" she asked. "I've only seen one once and that's the one I based the sketch off of." She wasn't sure how to respond to the mage's reaction to her sketch. Most people who spotted it simply glanced away, likely due to lack of recognition, but Remy's reaction was strongly negative.

"Terrible is what they are." Remy shook his head in disgust. "I hope to never come across one. For your sake, I hope you don't, either. They're used to steal a mage's power." He took his withheld bite and chewed slowly before adding, "they're very dangerous but thankfully they're very rare, too." He continued to explain that the last time one had even been heard of in the Inland Empire had been more than ten years previously.

Wendi stared at him, wide-eyed. "So the man who had it was a mage?" she asked. "Using someone else's magic?" If it had been that long since anyone had seen a trapping stone, it stood to reason that she hadn't come across one in her travels and that nobody had seemed to recognize it.

"No," He shook his head. "Nothing like that. It doesn't let the thief use the magic; it just locks it away so that the mage who originally owned the power can't use any of it.

"It's like a curse and a very dangerous thing to use. Done incorrectly, it can seriously hurt or even kill the mage it steals from."

Wendi considered his words. If what Remy said was true, that could have serious implications on her search for answers. "If someone survived this curse," she said after a long pause, "could it result in memory loss?" She was careful to keep her voice low and even, belying the fear that continued to build within her chest.

"Absolutely."

Her blood ran cold at his words, hardly believing what she was hearing. "What about physical defects? Could it do something like that?" She resisted the urge to reach up and touch the scar that ran along her face.

He thought for a moment before answering. "I suppose," he said finally. "Might depend on what kind of defects you're talking about but it would stand to reason that it could have some sort of physical effect on the body. I could see someone losing an arm, a leg, or even an eye if it was used on them."

21

Wendi was quiet for the rest of the meal. Conversation turned back to more mundane subjects and she was able to uphold her end of the conversation but only barely. As soon as Analisse and Remy left, she headed down to her lab. Too much had happened in her mind too quickly and she needed some time to digest all of it. Her lab was the best place for her to sort through all of the thoughts fluttering around inside her head and she did her best thinking while she was alone.

"Was I really a mage?" she asked herself, voice shaky with worry. She could hardly imagine it was true, but Remy had been very clear and precise in his identification of the trapping stone. There was another reason to believe she had once been a mage, after all. The pirate leader himself had said that he had taken her power, was that what he had meant? When he had first said it, Wendi hadn't understood but the meaning, assuming she wasn't completely misunderstanding everything, was becoming clearer by the moment.

"Were my powers stolen?"

Even more, she thought as she caught her black-eyed reflection in a glass decanter, Remy had said that bad things, horrible things, could happen to the targeted mage if the stone was used incorrectly. Was that what had happened to her memories, her facial scars, her eyes?

"He said it could cause memory loss and perhaps physical defects."

Did all of this happen because of the pirate's trapping stone? Had he been the one to do this to her?

If that was the case, she let the thoughts travel to their natural conclusion, what else had the stone changed on her? And how had it been done to her, been stolen from her in the first place?

"Better yet," she realized, "why?" Why steal her magic, if she had truly had magic to begin with. Why her? Had she done something, perhaps something so terrible that the stone had been used as a form of punishment? Or, and she wasn't sure if the thought was better or worse, had she just been a random target, an easy mark for the thief to steal magic from?

She quickly dismissed the last thought. Remy had been clear on that point when he said it didn't allow the pirate to use stolen magic, it simply kept the target from using theirs. There would be no point in stealing magic from a stranger, if that was the case. The only conclusion she could draw was that she had somehow known the pirate. But who was he? How had she known him?

Questions piled atop another in her mind and she couldn't write enough in her notes to keep them all in place. By the time she had put one question into ink, three more had popped up in its place. She slammed her fist against the paper on her desk, hoping that the shock would snap her back out of it, to no avail.

Perhaps, she considered, the removal of her magic was the very reason why she had discovered nothing about who she had been. If she had done something awful, committed some heinous crime, maybe a part of her punishment was that she was to never find out who and what she had been. The idea made sense, after all. If she truly had been a mage, someone would have known about her and heard about her disappearance.

Her flurry of thoughts inevitably returned to the pirate who had started the mental maelstrom. Remy had said that the stone was both very dangerous and very rare. Very rare almost always translated into very expensive in her world, making it an expensive item indeed for the pirate to have had in his possession.

He may have lied about being the one responsible for stealing her magic. "If that's the case," she wondered, "then how did he get the stone?" If she could trace how the pirate had gotten the stone, she might have an idea of her own whereabouts at the time it was used as well. She couldn't imagine that a trapping stone would just be discarded after use, so someone, somewhere, had to know from where he had gotten it. More importantly, they would know *when* he had gotten it, potentially narrowing down her own search period.

"That means maybe there is a way to undo all this." If the stone was used to trap any magic she had once had, then perhaps it could be used again to release the trapped magic. The thought gave her a glimmer of hope, hope she hadn't felt in a long time.

Along with the hope came suspicion. Was that why Phemie had been so accepting of her? Did her best friend already know the truth? The idea that Phemie could have known all about her and had let her exist in misery for the last five years brought her paranoid thoughts back into order in a way that pain hadn't been able. She knew her friend. There was absolutely no way that Phemie could do something like that to her.

"Not a chance. She's not like that."

Her thoughts were interrupted by a knock at her door. She glanced up in surprise as it opened and Sean walked into the room.

"I wanted to see how you were doing," he explained when she warily watched him enter. "Nothing more than that. You just looked really upset when the mages left, so I wanted to make sure I hadn't overstepped by going to get them."

"No," she reassured him as she scooped up her notes. "It was fine and I appreciate you saving me the trouble. I know I should have thanked you earlier but things have been kind of hectic." She took a deep breath and added, "And I may have overreacted yesterday, too. I know that you were trying to help but I'm still pretty upset over letting that guy escape."

Particularly so now that she had a couple more clues about the meaning of the necklace he had been wearing. If she hadn't let the pirate escape, she might have been able to get it away from him and possibly find a way to release the trapped magic.

"I overheard a part of what the mages were saying over dinner but I didn't understand all of it. Does that weird necklace drawing have something to do with whatever's going on with you?"

Wendi looked at him for a long moment before nodding. "I don't know how to explain everything to you in a way that would make sense. Right now, I can barely even make sense of it to myself."

Phemie bustled into the room before she could add anything further. She didn't have her usual chair and looked a little more harried than usual. "What she's trying to say," she looked between Wendi and Sean, "is that she just discovered she used to be a mage. Her power was stolen and locked in the amulet that evil little man was wearing yesterday."

Wendi looked at her friend, surprised and a little suspicious. *Had Phemie been listening in on the conversation too?* she wondered. Of course, her thoughts also returned to the idea that there was a conspiracy to keep her from discovering who she had been before she was Wendi. She had already dismissed the idea that Phemie could be involved in a cover-up like that but now it was starting to look like she had been mistaken to dismiss suspicion so quickly.

"Oh," Phemie dismissed Wendi's cautious look with a wave of her hand. "I've known for a long time now that you must have had some pretty powerful magic at some point." She smiled at Wendi wryly. "I suspected that it had been locked away somehow, but you never mentioned it so I didn't want to upset you by bringing it up."

"But..." Wendi tried to straighten the jumble of thoughts again. "Why didn't you tell me what that amulet was when I asked you about it? When I put the sketches of it up all over the place?"

"I didn't know," she admitted, both shoulders raised. "I didn't have the formal training your friends Remy and Analisse had, so I don't know about every magical trinket that's out there."

Her explanation made a lot of sense to Wendi. The Academy at Three Rivers was an expensive place for an aspiring mage to train so the only people who were able to study there were those who could afford the enrollment costs, people who usually came from well-to-do families. As far as she knew. Phemie didn't have any more family than Wendi herself did.

"If I had known," Phemie added gently, "I would have told you immediately. And if I'd known you didn't know you used to be a mage, I would have told you that, too."

"But how did you know I used to be a mage?" Wendi asked. "If all my power was taken, how could you tell?"

"Your eyes," she said. "Magic like what you used leaves a mark on the body and your eyes are the clearest sign of a necromancer I've ever seen."

Phemie's words may as well have been a physical blow, knocking Wendi from her seat. If her stool hadn't been so close to one of her cupboards, she would have tumbled all the way to the floor in shock. As it was, she had to grab onto the edge of her workbench to keep herself from falling completely. "A sign of what?" She had to have heard that incorrectly. There was no way that she could have been a death mage, was there?

"You aren't an alchemist," Phemie reached over and patted her hand. "You're a necromancer."

22

"All magic takes a toll on the body," Phemie explained. "Healing magic steals a tiny amount of the caster's life force. That life is then transferred to the spell's target, causing the advanced healing rate that those type of arts are commonly used for. The true test of power for a healing mage, therefore, is the ability to replenish his or her own life force."

"Doesn't that heal on its own?" Wendi vaguely remembered hearing Phemie speak of something similar many years before. She resettled herself on her stool as she waited for more explanation.

"Yes. Everyone's life force, unless it is blocked by other means, will heal itself. But that's also where part of the problem lies. If its replenished too quickly, the mage's body is overburdened and contradictorily wears itself out trying to keep itself alive. Replenished too slowly, the mage's body cannot recover from the damage to itself during the casting process. At low levels, neither of these are life-threatening but unless enough time is given to rest between castings, there is an unavoidable cumulative effect."

"So that's why you only brew one potion at a time instead of making a whole batch, then?"

"Exactly." The witch nodded her agreement. "Much like how your alchemy works, my potions require almost none of my own life force in order to brew but it still extracts some. I don't like running low, so I limit how much I do in order to maintain energy levels high enough for my own comfort.

"The same philosophy holds true for an enchanter like Remy. They imbue items with a small portion of themselves, not the life force that a healer uses but instead something similar known as the auric force. This portion of the mage's auric field is placed inside the enchanted item and manipulated to produce the intended result. The auric field, just as with the life force, needs to be replenished for the enchanter to survive.

"With all varieties of magic, the more powerful a spell is, the more of the caster is traded in the process. That's actually why some mages can only learn a handful of spells while others can learn as many as they want to; it all depends on their ability to replenish and how much life or auric field they have to begin with. Again, there are exceptions to almost everything but nobody can cast a spell that costs more than however much of their force the mage has available.

"Whether it is the caster's life force, the enchanter's auric force, or the diviner's mental force, an amount of the mage's force is extended every time they cast a spell."

"Is that why magic users often look older than they actually are?" Sean interrupted.

Phemie nodded. "Many mages who use the most powerful spells extend too much of themselves without the ability to adequately replenish it and they burn out. These mages appear used up, dried out, and, in a word, old."

"Does that mean I'm actually a lot younger than I thought I was?" Wendi asked.

Phemie shook her head. "Not necessarily. Truly powerful mages don't burn out as quickly as the rest. They have the ability to replenish themselves and, in many cases, can actually stunt their own aging process. By so doing, a powerful mage can appear much younger than he or she truly is."

"So I could be older, then?" She wasn't sure whether that possibility was better or worse than the idea of her being younger than she had believed.

"Again, not necessarily. Necromancy is different than all of the other varieties of magic. Practitioners of the death arts are more..." she searched for a word and failed. "Parasitic, I guess would be the best term, than other mages. Rather than using their own energies to cast their spells, they have the ability to tap into the life energies of others around them. Because of that, they aren't naturally prohibited from expending more than their own life force in energy.

"Some of the most powerful and dangerous necromancers known to exist have the ability to kill with a touch, draining the whole life force out of another living being. They can then use this force to cast spells, replenish their own personal energy, or to do as they wish. Only a truly evil necromancer kills using this or any similar method without using the energy he or she has taken.

"However, as with all other forms of magic, necromancy takes its toll on the body. Because they cast by taking from another, effectively stealing life, their own bodies reflect the death toll that they caused onto another being."

"So for me to look like this," Wendi gestured towards her eyes and the scar along the side of her face, "I had to have killed people?" She couldn't imagine herself killing even one person, let alone the quantity of people Phemie had indicated it would require for her eyes to be so dark. How could that even be possible?

"I don't know. I have no idea who you were or what you did before we met in the woods."

For over five years, Wendi had searched the country to find out who she was, where she was from, and how she had ended up looking the way she did. She had traveled from one end of the Inland Empire to the other, crossed over slightly into both of the neighboring empires to the north and south, and found nothing. Now, she had discovered that at least some of the answers she had been seeking had been right in front of her all along and she would give everything to have not discovered that particular truth. From what Phemie had just described, she would have had to kill a lot of people in order to receive that kind of damage. How many had perished at her hands? Tens? Hundreds? She didn't even want to contemplate the possibility of higher numbers. It was simply inconceivable.

She reflected back on her idea that nobody had reported her missing because she hadn't been missed. If what Phemie said was true, then it wasn't quite that she wasn't missed. If anything, people had celebrated her disappearance. Perhaps it was really a direct result of her own actions that had led to the trapping of her magic. Had someone used it in order to save themselves from her? Rather than being the victim in the whole thing, was she the antagonist?

Wendi was crushed by the news. Could she have really done all of this to herself? "There must be a way to fix it." She looked at her friend pleadingly. "Isn't there?"

"There's no way to reverse it," Phemie shook her head sadly. "There are ways to mitigate further damage but what's been done is already done. Even if we took you to the most powerful healer in all the empires, nothing would change."

Sean had been unusually silent during most of the women's conversation, his eyes darting back and forth between them, his skin growing paler with each new revelation. Appalled at the news even more than Wendi was, he finally pushed himself to his feet and stepped past both women to leave. His boots thundered up the stairs as he ran. From the sound, he took the steps two at a time, so great was his hurry to escape.

"Aren't you going to stop him?" Phemie asked quietly as his footsteps faded into the distance.

"No," Wendi shook her head, her voice barely above a whisper. "He's not a prisoner here; he never has been. He can leave any time he wants to." If anything, she was surprised he had waited so long to run.

"Now he just has more reason than ever to go."

23

Although part of her mystery had been solved, Wendi still had plenty of questions that remained unanswered. Who was the man with the necklace, really? She could have kicked herself as she pulled out a fresh sheet of parchment. Why hadn't she thought to draw him for a wanted poster when she had sketched the necklace? Now, her memories were even hazier due to the passage of time and she couldn't quite get his features right.

Could she be sure that he was the person who had trapped her power? He certainly seemed to be. He had been very self-assured, in a way that demonstrated he was used to holding power over other people.

"But why?" If he had been the person to steal her power, then what had been his reason? He had mentioned needing her services again. Did that mean that she had actually worked with the slick, smarmy dung-heap?

What did he want from her now? The only thing he had mentioned specifically was the Horn of Ascension but he had said he wanted her as well as the artifact. What more could he possibly want from her? It wasn't exactly as if she still had magic at her disposal for him to somehow force her to use.

The most important question was the one that she refused to give any time at all to. Each time it popped into her thoughts, she shoved it away as ruthlessly as she could but it kept returning.

Was Sean coming back?

Frustrated, she dug through page after page of notes, trying to find anything that she had overlooked before. There had to be a clue in all that she had gathered somewhere but she hadn't seen it, or at least hadn't realized its implications. She couldn't imagine that five years' worth of research could have turned up absolutely nothing.

She was also more determined than ever to figure out where the Horn of Ascension was and get her hands on it. That search had become almost as personal to her as finding out about her past. She didn't want it for her shop anymore. When she did find it, she wouldn't offer it up for sale. Chances were, she wouldn't even let anyone know that she had unearthed it. No, she wanted the Horn just to keep the pirate from getting it. He had taken something important from her and now she wanted to take something important from him. It was that simple.

Of course, simple was a relative term. It was simple to decide that she wanted the Horn and it was just as simple to decide that the man who had stolen her magic, no matter what his motivation for doing so had been, would not get it. Finding and acquiring the Horn, on the other hand, was a much more difficult matter.

Every time she heard bootsteps coming down the stairs, she looked up hopefully. To her disappointment, it had always been Phemie, bringing her something to eat or Jaegar, offering to bring her down more supplies. Occasionally it was Crucian, coming down just to check on her or to ask for more snakewine.

It was never the person she hoped it would be.

"You need to leave the lab sometime," Phemie had pointed out when bringing her lunch. Remnants of her breakfast, barely touched, still sat on the tray where they had been delivered. "This isn't going to help you get him back at all."

"There is no getting him back," Wendi had replied, far more angrily than she had meant to. "He was never mine to begin with, no matter what you wanted to see. He's gone and that's all there is to it."

"Fine," Phemie had snapped at her in return. "Don't go after him. But at the very least you need to come up into the air once in a while. Take a meal at the tavern. Go on another hunt for something to bring back for the menagerie or more information about whatever has you so obsessed. But don't just sit down here like a hermit and expect anything to happen."

"Fine," Wendi snapped in return. "I'll just go on my rounds and see if I can find out anything about that pirate jerk that led the attack on us."

Phemie nodded sharply. "You do that. And bring back some more Greystone mead while you're out."

That conversation had been more than a week earlier. It had taken Wendi almost that long to realize how badly she had needed Phemie to come down and throw her out of her laboratory, to get her up and moving again. She felt badly about fighting with her friend that way but she knew that Phemie understood. Even if she didn't, she would apologize when she got home.

At every town she had stopped on her trip, she asked questions, seeking information about the man who had attacked her. Some of the towns recognized her description of him and their explanations about who he had claimed to be ranged from travelling merchant to aspiring loremaster to a man seeking refuge from the civil war in the Dracott Empire. At each town, the stories changed and Wendi didn't believe a single one of them.

She also made quiet inquiries to see if any of the towns knew of a necromancer who may have disappeared some time ago. There, again, she didn't find much. When she stopped at Three Rivers to make inquiries at the Academy, she realized that she had to be much more careful in her explanations and questions.

There, she was directed to see Andress, one of the magi. Magi were the senior mages who instructed the young students in the magical arts, well versed in multiple fields of study. He was a lean gentleman in his late fifties, at least visually, but she suspected that he was much, much older in truth. "So why do you want to know about a missing necromancer?" he asked pleasantly as he offered her a seat in his office. His desk and shelves were covered with almost as many scrolls and tools as her lab beneath Dragon Keep was. The only thing that was missing were all of the components and she didn't keep a set of mages robes in her lab like the ones hanging from a hook behind him. "You must understand that it is a very unusual line of inquiry."

"I came across an item called a trapping stone recently." His light brown eyes widened behind large round glasses and he leaned his head forward, obviously taken aback by her statement. "It was owned by a man who claimed to have trapped someone's magic in it and I want to know the identity of the necromancer from whom it was stolen."

"A trapping stone," he breathed. "Those are extremely dangerous. Did he give you any information beside that?"

She shook her head. "All I have been able to piece together so far is that it happened at least five but possibly more years ago and that the target had been a necromancer." She hoped her voice wasn't shaking as she explained; she needed to at least appear calm and collected in front of the magi, even if it was the opposite of how she felt inside. If her heart was to beat any more loudly, she was sure, he would be able to hear it.

"You must understand," Andress leaned forward, elbows on his knees, fingers interlaced below his chin, "that using a trapping stone is no small feat. Most mages are heavily warded against such attempts to usurp their power, so it would take a skilled and devious person to even make an attempt, let alone to succeed in it."

"I understand that," Wendi explained, "but I have reason to believe that it happened nonetheless, and that it was done inexpertly."

Andress raised an eyebrow at that and Wendi realized that she wasn't going to get anything of value out of the mage unless she gave him more information in return. He probably already had some suspicions, she thought as she remembered that Phemie had known Wendi was a mage even before she had.

Slowly, terrified of how the mage would react, she lowered her head, reached up, and lifted her hood away from her face. As it fell back onto her shoulders, she lifted her telltale eyes to meet his. "I can remember five years," she explained, her voice quavering. "Before that, nothing."

He closed his eyes and rubbed the bridge of his nose for a moment before speaking further. "I can't imagine how difficult this must be for you. Not only to have your magic taken away but for your memories to be taken as well. I understand that the use of a trapping stone is likely to kill the target, so the mere fact that you remain alive is quite the testament. I know it is but small consolation but the loss of one's memories pales in comparison to the loss of one's life."

"Up until just a couple weeks ago," she explained, "I had no idea what I was or that I had ever been anything but an alchemist. I had no idea why my eyes were black; I just knew that there was something wrong with me and that I needed to keep them hooded to keep from scaring everyone around me."

"There is nothing wrong with you, my dear." He reached out and took one of her hands in his aged one. "People fear what they do not understand."

He sighed and added, "Unfortunately, I don't know who you are other than who you are right now. I haven't heard anything about a trapping stone being used for well over a hundred years now. Furthermore, the necromantic arts are highly illegal in this region, so even if you had been from nearby, you likely would have kept your identity quite secret."

That made a lot of sense to her. If she had kept herself hidden away due to her abilities, it would explain why she couldn't find much information about herself. Not that it helped much in her quest. Crestfallen, she nodded that she understood and retrieved her hand. "Thank you for your time," she said flatly. "If there is anything I can do to assist you in the future, please don't hesitate to let me know." Disappointment filled her eyes with tears and she lifted her hood and turned to leave before they escaped.

She continued to travel around the transport gate network, checking for information at every town that she came across. At all of them, she found more descriptions of the blue-eyed pirate but nobody seemed to know who he truly was other than increasing rumors of his being the pirate king. The latest news didn't surprise her, given what she had personally witnessed of his interactions with the other pirates during their assault on her keep. If that had been done on his orders, it only added more facts to support the theory.

Finally, there was only one town left in the network that she hadn't yet been to and she spent almost three hours in her favorite tavern in Hub, convincing herself to go.

Word had already reached her about Sean's impending marriage. Most of the Inland Empire was abuzz with the news that the scion of the McClannahan family had finally selected a woman to be his bride. Wendi gritted her teeth as she heard the excitement that everyone but she seemed to be feeling about the event. The last thing she wanted to do was see the happy pair together, as she knew they would be. But Hoem was where McClannahan Trading was based and the Temptress was in town, which meant that John was as well.

She didn't have much of a choice.

There was simply nowhere else available to look.

Wendi was not yet in town for so much as an hour before the perky girl spotted her. "If you're here for the wedding," Hethere said as she sauntered over to her, "you might as well just turn around and leave. You aren't invited."

"What makes you think I'd want to come to your wedding?" Wendi responded coldly, refusing to rise to the girl's bait. "I'm here on business." Not wanting to cause a scene, she turned to walk away.

"I don't know why you even bother to wear that ridiculous hood," Hethere taunted her. "Sean already told everyone what kind of a freak you really are."

She should have expected as much. After all, there was no reason for Sean to not tell people everything he had learned. Still, her words stung, cutting far deeper than Hethere could have imagined. Snarling, Wendi whirled on the infuriating girl. "Frankly, I'm surprised that Mayor McClannahan is willing to let someone like you marry his precious son. Does Sean know how many beds you were warming while he was working for me?"

Wendi had no way of knowing whether her words were true or not but by Hethere's reaction, she suspected that she had touched a nerve.

Serves her right, she thought to herself. She had long since run out of patience for just about everything.

"Throw stones at me," she said almost inaudibly, "and I'll bury you under boulders."

Screeching in rage, Hethere launched at Wendi with her claw-sharp fingernails. She only managed to take half a step, however, before she was yanked backward by her head. A small, dark-haired woman, dressed in black with a satin eyepatch covering her left eye and a pair of viciously hooked swords attached to her hips, had one hand tangled in Hethere's hair, pulling her down and off-balance. The armed woman looked displeased about where her hand was, as though she had touched something foul.

A young red-haired man, another member of the McClannahan family no doubt, stood nearby. A wide grin played across his face as he laughed with glee, whether at Wendi's remark or at Hethere's predicament, she couldn't tell.

The smaller woman leaned forward to whisper something quietly into Hethere's ear. Hethere, in turn, went pale and nodded sullenly. As soon as she was released, Hethere turned to leave, shooting a murderous glance at all three of them as she walked away.

24

"I assume you don't remember me," the small woman said as she looked up at Wendi. "My name is Jasika and this is Keagan."

"No," Wendi agreed as she looked between the pair. "I'm sorry, but I have no idea who you are."

"Wait," Keagan said as he finally managed to catch his breath. He looked at Jasika expectantly. "What did you say to her?"

Jasika shrugged. "I simply informed her that if I caught her being rude to another guest of our town, she'd wake up in Oree's bed instead of Sean's on her wedding morning."

Keagan burst into a fresh fit of giggles but Wendi looked at Jasika as though she were mad. "Why would you do something like that?" Wendi asked incredulously. "Oree doesn't deserve to be treated that badly." Keagan's laughter increased at that and a faint smile flickered across Jasika's face, disappearing again so quickly Wendi had to wonder if she had imagined it.

"Oree might be offended but I can handle that. And I really doubt Sean would care much, he doesn't particularly like her anyway." To Wendi's surprise, Jasika took a swift step forward, stopping directly in front of her. The woman moved like a hunter, she realized. She had never seen anyone move with such grace and precision, or so quickly, without appearing to move at all. Even Oree's snakelike movements were clumsy in comparison. Jasika reached up and lifted the edge of Wendi's hood slightly, enough to be able to peer underneath but not enough to display her features for all to see. Nodding silently to herself, she released the fabric and stepped back again.

140

"You're looking for Tuan," she said simply.

"Who's Tuan?" Wendi asked, but the name seemed strangely familiar. So, in fact, did the small woman before her. If only she knew why.

"He's the one that attacked you in your keep a short time ago," Jasika answered. "Unless the descriptions and sketches are mistaken."

"You know who he is?" Wendi would have stepped closer in eagerness but something about Jasika's stance and demeanor told her that would be a very bad idea. "Tell me, please."

"I think this discussion should be held somewhere a little more private," Jasika answered. "Keagan and I were on our way to Cookie's for lunch. Would you care to join us?"

Cookie had to stop the trio as they walked into the restaurant. He hugged Jasika warmly, which she accepted although it was obvious she wasn't used to such affections. After rubbing his knuckles across Keagan's head, he hugged Wendi as well, to her surprise. "It's good to see you again," he said seriously to her.

"We need to talk privately for a few minutes if you don't mind," Jasika pointed out. "Could we all get a table in the back and some steamer pots?"

Unfazed by Jasika's abrupt manner, Cookie nodded. "Go ahead and have a seat. I'll bring the pots to you when they're done."

"Tuan was my guildmaster in Rex," Jasika explained once the three of them were seated and alone. "Considering how much you've been travelling around to other towns and asking about him, his amulet, and a missing person who sounds suspiciously similar to you, I assume you lost at least some of your memories when your magic was taken away from you."

Wendi nodded. "I don't remember anything." Jasika visibly winced at her admission, leading her to ask why.

"I guessed as much. If you hadn't lost your memories, you wouldn't have spent so much time asking about things you should already know about.

"I hadn't realized that would happen," she said with a sigh. "It was just supposed to take your power, not your memories too." She closed her eyes before adding, "Had I known what it was going to do to you, I would never have agreed to do it."

Wendi sat quietly, letting her words sink in. The last thing she had expected to find on this trip, and particularly in this location, was the person who had stolen her magic. She wanted to hate Jasika, to blame her for what she had done to her, but it seemed as though she was truly repentant for what she had caused.

"Why?" she asked finally. "Why did you do it?"

"I had orders," Jasika shrugged one shoulder. "I worked for Tuan; I was loyal to him. I didn't question when he gave me an assignment, I just did as I was instructed."

"Is there any way to reverse it?" If Jasika had taken her magic, then perhaps she would know of a way to give it back to her. Her hopes fell as Jasika shook her head helplessly.

"If there is a way to reverse it, I don't know about it," she admitted. "I might be able to check with some of my contacts but I can't guarantee how successful I'll be in that." She continued to explain that the magic was still trapped in the stone and as long as Tuan had it, she doubted that Wendi would regain the use of her power.

Wendi wasn't sure that she wanted her magic back but she was positive that she didn't want to let Tuan, if that really was his name, have even this victory over her. He may have gotten her magic taken away from her but by the gods she was going to take it back. Even if she couldn't use it, she wanted the skull-shaped medallion.

It was hers.

"There is another thing you've been searching for," Jasika broke into her thoughts. "The Horn of Ascension."

"Yes," Wendi replied absently. "That man, Tuan, came into my shop looking for it and it made me curious. From what I can understand, it's part of the Dracott Empire's royal regalia. Now, I want it just to keep him from having it." She looked at Jasika and Keagan sheepishly. "Petty, I know, but it's true."

"I think it would be a good idea for you to stop looking for it," Jasika said pointedly. "It's perfectly safe and Tuan will never get his hands on it again."

"So he really did have it at one time?" Wendi hadn't been sure whether she had believed that portion of Tuan's claims, but this was the first time she had been able to verify it. "Does that mean he's from one of the ruling houses of the Dracott Empire?"

"No," Jasika was quick to reassure her. "He stole it, after all that's what thieves do. I think he wants to take control of the Dracott Empire but he'll never get the chance so long as I'm alive."

Wendi looked between Jasika and Keagan curiously. It seemed as though both of them knew far more about the Horn of Ascension than they were letting on but she was hesitant to ask for more details. She had already learned far more than she had hoped to find.

Once their meal was complete, Jasika and Keagan left Wendi alone at the table with her thoughts. Wendi was thankful for the moment of solitude. She had a lot of things to think about and, apparently, a few new decisions to make.

"How are you doing?" Oree interrupted her musing. Without waiting for an invitation, he slipped down into the seat that Keagan had vacated. Wendi had almost forgotten that Cookie was Oree's grandfather, so it made sense for him to be at Cookie's restaurant. She suspected that helping out in the kitchen had taken up a good portion of Oree's time since his return to Hoem, if for no other reason than to keep him from getting into further trouble.

"Better than some, worse than others, I'd guess," she said as she looked across the table at him. "It's nice to see you again. I hope you've been well."

"I have," he reassured her. "Hannibal, too." He eyed her thoughtfully for a long moment before getting to the point. "I think you should go talk to Sean."

"Why would I want to do that?" she asked. "He made it pretty clear that he wants nothing more to do with me or anyone else from my keep."

"Because if you don't," Oree looked pleadingly at her, "I think he might actually go through with this ridiculous wedding, just because he's a stubborn idiot."

She had to smile faintly at that. Never one to mince words, Oree could be relied on to call a spade a spade. "I don't think that'd be a very good idea."

"Better than letting him marry that little social climber." Oree's brows furrowed as he spoke. "Both Hannibal and I have already tried to talk to him but he won't listen to either of us."

"And what makes you think he'd listen to me?" she asked. "He hates me."

"He doesn't hate you," he answered. "He likes you and he definitely respects you. If you went to talk to him, he'd be more likely to hear you out than either of us."

Sadly, Wendi shook her head. "I don't think I can help you in this. Sean's all grown up now and he can make his own decisions. If those decisions involve getting married to a vain little self-important twit, that's his prerogative."

"He's an idiot," Oree repeated. "And he needs someone who'll tell him that every now and again instead of just pandering to his ego. If you tell him to stop being such a jerk and to look at what he's about to do, he'll listen to you before he ruins his life."

"That's not my decision to make," she said as she stood to leave. "It's his." She dropped a handful of coins on the table, more than enough to cover her meal, and walked quietly out of the restaurant.

25

Two days later, Wendi found herself returning to Hoem. A runner from McClannahan Trading had arrived that morning with a list of goods from the Temptress.

"Captain John wasn't sure what you would be interested in," the runner had explained. "He said it might be better if you came to see for yourself."

Kicking herself for not going to see John like she had intended to do the last time she had been in town, which would have made a second trip unnecessary, she headed for the transport gate. As she walked out of the shop, she stopped at the doorway and threw the attraction philter that Phemie had sneaked into her pocket back at the witch.

"This is business," she pointed out calmly but firmly. "Save that for someone who wants one."

Unfazed, Phemie caught the philter and settled it back onto the counter where it belonged.

Wendi looked neither left nor right as she walked briskly from the gate in Hoem to the docks. There were plenty of places in town where she could have stopped, people she could have said hello to but she wanted to see John, purchase what she wanted from his hold, and then get back home before running into anyone she didn't want to see.

"Good afternoon," she greeted Dane when she saw him. It hadn't been until recently that she had discovered that Dane was also a Mc-Clannahan; his fair hair had been misleading.

"And a fine one it is," he agreed, smiling broadly at her. "I'll let John know you're here and he can take you down to the cargo area." He offered her a hand onto the ship, steadying her against the slow sway of the boat as it rocked with the motion of waves coming in from the sea.

She stood on the deck, looking around in wonder. She had only been on a couple of ships before but none of them had been as large or as clean as this one was. The Temptress had a wide stretch of wooden deck in the center with raised decks at both the front and rear. It even had a figurehead, a carved representation of a beautiful woman stretching out from its bow. From what she had witnessed of other trading ships, a figurehead was a rare sight indeed.

"Wendi," John's powerful voice greeted her as he arrived on the deck. He strode toward her, long strides that didn't seem to mind the movement of the floor beneath him, a testament to the amount of time he spent on board and his ease on the water. He took one of her hands in his own rough, calloused ones and shook it heartily. "I hadn't expected you to arrive so quickly."

"I had time," she explained, "and I wanted to be sure to get here before all the good finds had already been found." She smiled at him. Despite his gruff demeanor and imposing stature, she liked the man.

"In that case, you got here just in time," his eyes twinkled at her. She couldn't tell if he was smiling beneath his grizzled beard or not but even if his lips were flat, his eyes revealed his amusement. "I have some things set aside that I thought you might find to be of particular interest."

He led her down to the cargo hold, the vast room beneath the ship's main deck where all of his trading goods were stored. Crates and casks lined the wall, held in place with long lengths of netting. A pair of paths led from one end of the hold to another, granting access to peruse the three stacks of goods.

There was fresh bitterbeer from Greystone, some carved banana palm trinkets and fresh mangoes from Aquos and an assortment of implements carved from whale bones purchased in Burgard. There were a lot of other items that she had less interest in such as silk cloth from Tradewinds, piles of fur from Vanguard and carved wooden beads from Dive but none of those would be carried in her shop. Interesting as they were, they were too mundane for her customers.

For herself, however, she found a nice pelt of winter wolf that would make an excellent blanket during the upcoming snow season. Although the main building at Dragon Keep was restored, it was still a little bit breezy and the winters got quite cold, particularly at night when the hearth-fires ran low.

As an afterthought, she added a ream of the silk to her purchases. She had no idea what she would use it for but she was sure she could come up with something. If nothing else, she liked the feel of the fabric against her skin, so perhaps she would craft some new lounging pillows from it.

As much as she liked John personally, she truly enjoyed trading with him. He was stern and gruff for the most part but he was honest in his dealings, which was more than could be said about some of the other traders she dealt with on a regular basis. Wendi knew that the prices he quoted to her were the same prices he gave to other merchants. John didn't seem to believe, as so many others did, that a woman couldn't possibly be competent at running a business. So many merchants saw swindling her and overcharging her – or at least attempting to – as proof of their own superiority. There were a small handful of traders who she refused to do business with because of tactics such as those and she hadn't felt any compunction about informing them, once to a merchant in front of his customers, exactly why they wouldn't see another thaler from her.

As she loaded her purchases into her cart, John handed her an unmarked bottle. She accepted it but looked up at him questioningly.

"It's spicewine," he explained. "I was given a case of it at one of my stops and I need to know if there's a market for it before I agree to buy any more of it. Since your specialty is unusual stuff and you have a tavern in your keep, you were one of the first people I thought of to sample it. If you like it, let me know and I'll get some more for you."

"Thank you," she said, surprised by both his generosity and his thoughtfulness. "I'll let you know one way or another before you leave again." She turned back to her wagon to tuck the bottle securely among the rest of her purchases. When she looked back up, however, she discovered an unwelcome pair of people walking down the street towards her.

Sean looked up and spotted her immediately. Hethere, oblivious, continued to chatter away, one hand tucked possessively into his arm. Wendi couldn't hear what the obnoxious girl was saying but she wouldn't have cared if she had. She scowled and continued loading her wagon.

"What are you doing here?" Sean stormed over to her, glowering furiously. "Shouldn't you be off in your dungeon?"

"Preparing for your wedding banquet, of course," she snapped at him in return. "What does it look like I'm doing?"

He snapped back at her comment as though she had struck him. "You're just here to cause trouble, aren't you?" he accused. "Why can't you just go back home and leave the rest of us alone?"

"I'm working," she turned to face him. "It's called a job. I have responsibilities. You may have heard of those once or twice but I seriously doubt you've ever come into close contact with either."

He stepped closer, looming over her as he was prone to do when angered. "I paid my debt back to you," he growled. "I don't owe you anything."

"You paid me nothing," she disagreed. "You came to me, begging me to take you back, and I let you. I forgave your debt long ago." She had to tilt her head to look directly at him, he was so close to her. Her hood slipped as she moved, but she paid it no heed as it fell around her shoulders. "If anything, *you* were the one who couldn't go home and leave the rest of us alone."

"Sean," Hethere pulled on his arm to bring him away from her. "We're going to be late for your suit fitting. You need a proper outfit to wear to the ceremony tomorrow evening." The glare she shot at Wendi was pure malice.

Wendi smiled, as sweetly as she could, knowing exactly how much it infuriated Sean when she did. "Go on to your fripperies, you spoiled little boy," she said through clenched teeth, incapable of keeping her mouth closed. Her smile never faltered.

His eyes flashed and darkened, and she wondered if she had finally gone too far. One of his arms twitched as though he was about to strike her for her comment but he maintained control enough to turn his back on her and walk away.

Behind her, she could hear the echoes of snickering floating across the water. When she turned, she spotted both John and Dane, leaning against the dock's railing and laughing.

"I'm impressed," John said. "I've never seen anyone get that strong of a reaction out of Sean that quickly."

Dane had to pitch in his own thoughts. "If there had been any more sparks flying, we'd have to take cover."

Thoroughly unamused with the entire McClannahan family, Wendi cinched down the last of her straps, more firmly than she would normally have done, and headed home.

26

Wendi had been in a thoroughly rotten mood since her arrival back at Dragon Keep. She knew she was acting like a wounded bear and attacking everything that came within striking range but though she tried to stop it, she couldn't. Phemie, Crucian and Jaegar were all hiding from her and she couldn't blame them for it.

If she could, she would hide from her too.

She headed directly to her lab, determined to focus on what she knew would calm her before she lost control of herself completely. Two vats of gum were destroyed, as well as three vials of deathrattle antidote before she gave up. Even her work wasn't as soothing as it normally would have been, which was the first time that had ever happened to her.

She just couldn't concentrate.

She stalked up the stairs and into the store room, searching for something that would calm her mind. On one of the shelves, she spotted the bottle of spicewine John had given her. "I need to sample that anyway," she grumbled to herself. "Let's see how well it works."

She carried the bottle to her suite of rooms to drink herself into oblivion. If the spicewine wasn't enough to do the job, she figured, she could always grab a bottle of Greystone mead or the bitterbeer she had just purchased. That stuff was strong enough to knock even Jaegar off his feet.

Halfway through the bottle, which wasn't bad, she decided, she was interrupted by a knock on her door. Swearing profusely, she stomped across the room to see who had dared to interrupt her while she was in a bad mood. Whoever it was, she was positive, wouldn't make that mistake again soon.

As soon as she started to open it, the door was pushed open further as Hannibal and Oree pushed their way into her room. Sean, barely conscious, hung limply between them. "Hiya Wendi," Hannibal greeted her cheerfully as he and Oree hauled Sean across her room and dropped him, groaning, onto her bed.

He didn't look like he had been beaten, Wendi determined as she stepped closer to examine him, instantly sober. After only a cursory examination, she decided that he looked as though he had been drugged. Swearing again, she reached for the small package of antidotes in the drawer of her nightstand.

As she flipped the leather case open, Oree reached over and took the entire thing from her hands. "He'll be fine," he explained. His face was serious but showed none of the worry that she would have expected to find. Sean was one of his best friends and if he had been drugged, hadn't they brought him to her to be fixed?

"Sean will be fine in the morning," he explained at her worried look. "We just needed somewhere to hide him."

"Hide him?" She tried to comprehend what he was saying. "Who's looking for him? Is he in trouble?"

"He's fine," Hannibal chimed in, echoing Oree's previous assertion. "We kidnapped him."

"You what?" She looked between the two men and their prone friend. "Why would you do something like that?" Neither of them showed any shame for their actions. In fact, if she had to guess, they looked proud.

"Because he's an idiot," Oree reminded her. "If we hadn't, he would have actually gone through with the stupid wedding."

It was only then that Wendi realized that all three men were dressed in the fine clothing of a wedding party. Oree wore a dark green formal jacket with brass buttons over pale tan pants with an embroidered belt wrapped around his waist. Even his boots looked like they had been recently polished. Hannibal was dressed similarly but in pale blue. On the bed, Sean was dressed in a white jacket with golden buttons that she was positive were the same color as his hair.

There was far too much embroidery on the three men, she decided. None of them looked comfortable, perhaps with the exception of the barely-conscious Sean, and all of them looked overdressed.

"We would have just taken him to the inn," Hannibal supplied, "but Phemie insisted we bring him up here."

With not many other choices readily available, Wendi agreed that the trio could stay. Sean was fully unconscious by the time she had heard the entire story and after she checked to make sure he hadn't been dosed too strongly she went downstairs. No amount of alcohol was going to help her now. Instead, what she needed was to get some food in her stomach to absorb the wine she had imbibed.

As she walked toward the tavern, Keagan came jogging toward her from the gate. "I need to see the guys," he said as he approached her.

"Which guys?" she asked as she continued to walk.

"Sean, Oree and Hannibal."

She shook her head and walked into the tavern. As she signaled to Krun that she needed a meal, she said, "What makes you think I know where they are?"

"Look," Keagan said, exasperated. "I know they're here. All I need is to talk to Hannibal and Oree."

When she asked if he was there on Hethere's behalf, he grudgingly admitted that he was. "But not the way you're thinking," he was quick to point out. "She knows that they took Sean and she's threatening to destroy Oree's fishing boat if they don't give him back." He continued to explain that Hethere was livid at the disruption of her wedding. She knew that his friends had been behind his disappearance and if her fiancée wasn't returned to her by nightfall, Oree would find his boat at the bottom of the bay. "So you see," he finished, "there's not a lot of time left."

"Wait here," she sighed grudgingly. As much as she didn't want to send Sean back home to continue with the farce of a marriage, she didn't want to be responsible for the destruction of his friend's property. "I'll send them out shortly." She settled Keagan at a table and picked up her own plate, heading back to her suite.

There, she explained to the men about Keagan's arrival and the message he had brought. For a moment, it looked as though they would ignore the warning but finally Oree caved. Chagrined, he and Hannibal picked Sean back up to bring him back to his bride.

Before they left, however, Wendi stopped them. She picked her antidote kit up from the nightstand where Oree had left it and pulled out a vial.

If she was going to send him away to get married, she was going to make for absolute certain that he knew what he was doing. His eyes began to clear as she fed him the contents of the bottle, but she refused to meet them.

As soon as the bottle was empty, she stepped back to let them pass.

Once everyone was gone, Wendi went back into her room to finish the bottle of spicewine. Not that it mattered, she knew. No matter how much she drank, it wouldn't change anything. She flopped back on the bed, staring at the ceiling but even that was too much to bear. The heady, musky scent that was undeniably Sean filled her senses.

"I wonder if he's married yet," she wondered an hour later as she poured yet another glass of wine, torturing herself with the thought. She had no doubts that Hethere would have dragged him to the altar, even though Wendi wasn't sure Sean would have recovered completely from the drug's effects by the time his friends brought him back to her.

She imagined the ceremony, breathing in the scent of Sean that lingered where he had been placed on her bed and tears fell freely, unchecked and unceasing. He may be a jerk, she admitted, and he may be an idiot at times, but he deserved better than to marry that whiny little brat. No matter what redeeming qualities Hethere may have had, Wendi knew that she would never like Sean's wife.

Perhaps this was the way things were meant to be after all, she realized. Hethere was beautiful, only a blind man could miss noticing how attractive she was. How could a man like Sean not be happy, married to a girl who looked like that? She sniffled and sat up, looking for the bottle of spicewine to pour herself another glass.

As she poured, she caught her reflection in the dark bottle and fresh tears flowed. Nothing she had been able to piece together about her past had helped. In fact, it had only made things worse. She wasn't a person who had been missed when she disappeared and she certainly hadn't been accidentally transformed by an errant spell.

She was a monster.

She was the demon that everyone believed her to be.

She was a stealer of lives.

Needing to get away from Sean's essence, which seemed to permeate her room everywhere she went, she picked up her bottle and walked down to her lab. She sat among her poisons and distilled venoms, wondering how many lives it had taken to turn her eyes obsidian.

She put a hand against the side of her face, tracing the grooves of her scar. Who had paid the price for that, she wondered. Whatever she had gotten in return, had it been worthwhile?

She cried again at that, crying until she fell asleep. Tears for what she had done, tears for the unknown lives she had destroyed, and tears for what she had done to herself in the process.

But above all else, she cried for the one thing that she couldn't admit out loud. If she had her magic back, she knew that she would do it all over again.

She really was a monster.

27

She didn't hear the door to her lab open. When soft footsteps crossed the rough stone floor, she heard nothing. When the hand touched her shoulder, however, she jerked upright, instantly awake.

Sean stood beside her, still dressed in his wedding finery. She blinked absently at him for a moment, trying to determine whether or not she was in a dream. "What are you doing here?" she asked finally. "Shouldn't you be enjoying your wedding night?" Her cheeks were still wet, so she knew that she hadn't been asleep for long.

"I don't want to be like my uncle John," he explained. She looked at him in confusion, so he continued. "He has been married five times. He's attracted to a woman so he marries her almost as soon as he meets her. Gets divorced almost as quickly.

"He's been divorced five times, too. It never takes very long after he gets married to discover that he has nothing whatsoever in common with the woman he married and both of them end up angry and resentful over it."

Wendi watched him, curious about what he was trying to say but not wanting to interrupt. She had heard about John McClannahan's track record with marriages of course, almost everyone in the Inland Empire had heard about it. But she wasn't sure what John's failed marriages had to do with Sean.

"I know that's what would happen if I married Hethere," he said, stepping closer to her. "And I don't want to be that kind of a person. I don't want to destroy both her life and mine because I couldn't stand up to my parents.

"I told my mother that putting up with one spoiled brat was enough, that I wasn't going to marry another one just because she came from a good family. When I do get married, I want it to be because I found the person I can't live without." Gently, he reached out and took her hand, pulling her to her feet and holding her close to him. "And right now," he said, "I don't think I can live without you."

Before he could say anything further, however, she interrupted him. "You don't know anything about me. You don't know the kind of person I am. When you find out, you'll change your mind again and I don't want you to hate me for it when you discover the truth." Though she tried to blink them back, fresh tears began to fall as she spoke.

"I don't even know anything about me," she admitted quietly.

"I know enough about you to know that I'm staying right here," he replied. "Whether you agree to marry me or not, you're not getting rid of me so easily."

"But," she tried to think, but it wasn't easy with him so close. "I was a necromancer. You left when you found out."

"I know," he said, closing his eyes repentantly. "And I shouldn't have. It surprised me, I admit, and it scared me but I know that it doesn't matter." He opened his eyes and looked down at her, leaning forward to kiss her.

She leaned back, away from him. Not because she wanted to but because she had to if she wanted to think clearly. "I'm going to get my power back," she pointed out. "I don't know how to do it yet, but I will."

"Fine," he growled, becoming impatient at her refusal to let him kiss her. "I don't care. But if you're planning to go after the Pirate King to get that stupid necklace and your magic, you're going to need someone like me around.

"I've travelled pretty extensively, you know, and I know where to get information about a lot of things. Keagan and Jasika are willing to help, too. She feels pretty badly about having taken your magic to begin with and she wants a piece of Tuan anyway."

"But..." Her objections were stifled as he crushed her mouth beneath his. He pushed her back against her worktable, drinking her in as though he was dying of thirst and she was an oasis in the desert. Any thoughts of denying him were irrelevant, she realized.

"You're going to marry me eventually," he said when he finally pulled back.

"Why would I want to marry a spoiled brat like you?" she challenged him in return, more out of habit than actual refusal.

"Because I want you to," he growled as he held her even tighter. "And I always get what I want."

The adventure continues in

Grand Coven

available in 2024

Shanon L. Mayer is the author of multiple book series, including the Chronicles of the Chosen, the Inland Sea series and the Jen Rice series.

She was born in Portland, Oregon in 1978 and lived most of her life in the Pacific Northwest. She received a Bachelor of Arts in Business Administration from Washington State University in 2013, which did nothing to quench her passion for the fantasy genre.

9 781958 076057